AUG c 2008

INDIAN TRAILS
PUBLIC LIBRARY DISTRICT
WHEELING, ILLINOIS 60090
847-459-4100
www.Indiantrailslibrary.org

THE CREATURE
FROM THE DEPTHS

PROPERTY OF INDIAN TRAILS
PUBLIC LIBRARY DISTRICT

Adapted and Illustrated by
Mark Kidwell

Based upon the works of
H.P. Lovecraft

magic
Wagon

visit us at
www.abdopublishing.com

Published by Magic Wagon, a division of the ABDO Publishing Group, 8000 West 78th Street, Edina, Minnesota 55439. Copyright © 2008 by Abdo Consulting Group, Inc. International copyrights reserved in all countries. All rights reserved. No part of this book may be reproduced in any form without written permission from the publisher. Graphic Planet™ is a trademark and logo of Magic Wagon.

Printed in the United States.

Based upon the works of H.P. Lovecraft
Written & Illustrated by Mark Kidwell
Colored & Lettered by Jay Fotos
Edited & Directed by Chazz DeMoss
Cover Design by Neil Klinepier

Library of Congress Cataloging-in-Publication Data

Kidwell, Mark.
    The creature from the depths / written and illustrated by Mark Kidwell ; based upon the works of H.P. Lovecraft.
        p. cm. -- (Graphic Horror)
    ISBN-13: 978-1-60270-057-4 (reinforced lib. bnd. ed.)
    ISBN-10: 1-60270-057-5 (reinforced lib. bnd. ed.)
    1. Graphic novels. I. Lovecraft, H. P. (Howard Phillips), 1890-1937. II. Title.

PN6727.K483C74 2008
741.5973--dc22

                                                    2007002774

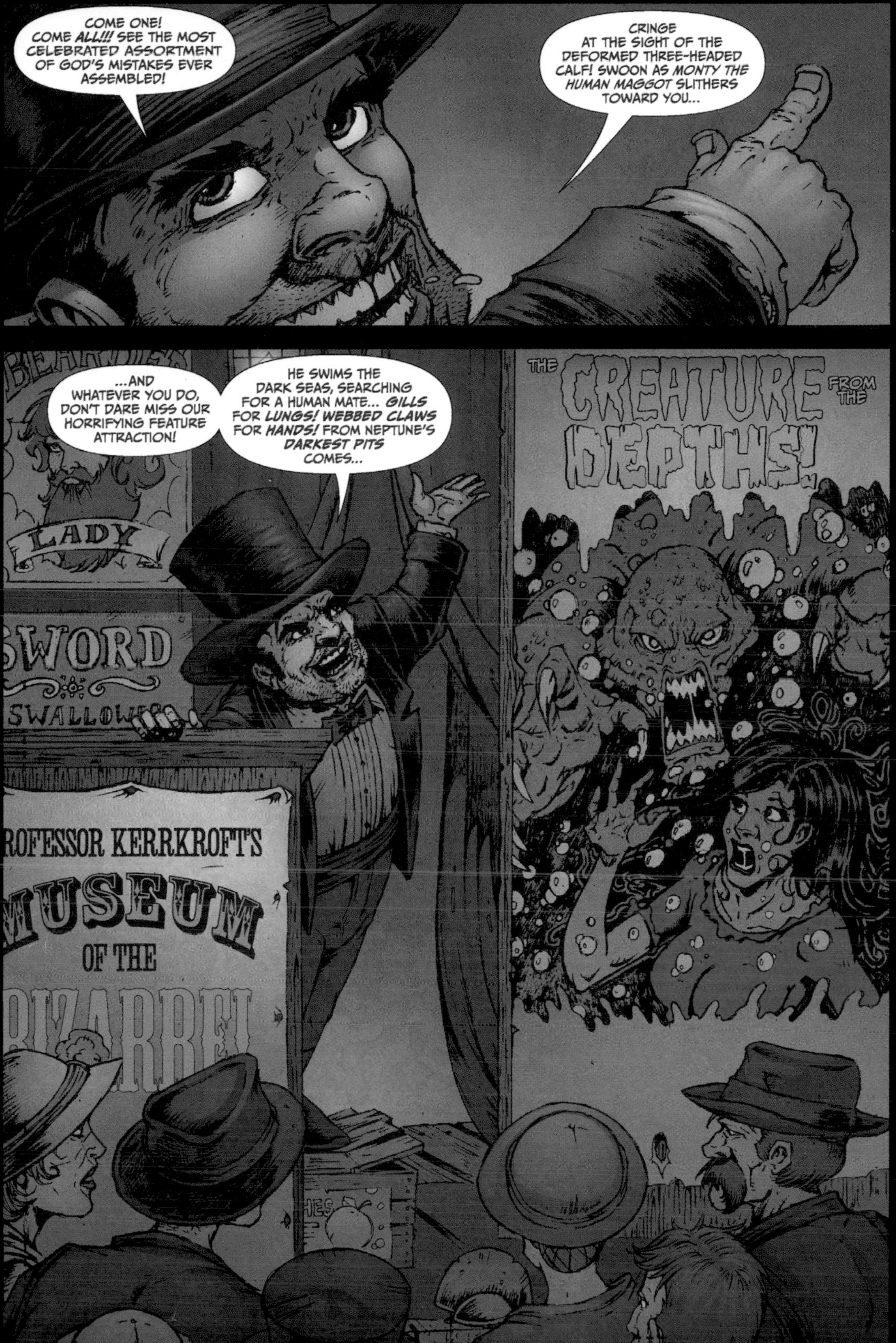
COME ONE! COME ALL!!! SEE THE MOST CELEBRATED ASSORTMENT OF GOD'S MISTAKES EVER ASSEMBLED!
CRINGE AT THE SIGHT OF THE DEFORMED THREE-HEADED CALF! SWOON AS MONTY THE HUMAN MAGGOT SLITHERS TOWARD YOU...
...AND WHATEVER YOU DO, DON'T DARE MISS OUR HORRIFYING FEATURE ATTRACTION!
HE SWIMS THE DARK SEAS, SEARCHING FOR A HUMAN MATE... GILLS FOR LUNGS! WEBBED CLAWS FOR HANDS! FROM NEPTUNE'S DARKEST PITS COMES...
THE CREATURE FROM THE DEPTHS!
LADY
SWORD
SWALLOW
ROFESSOR KERRKROFT'S
MUSEUM
OF THE

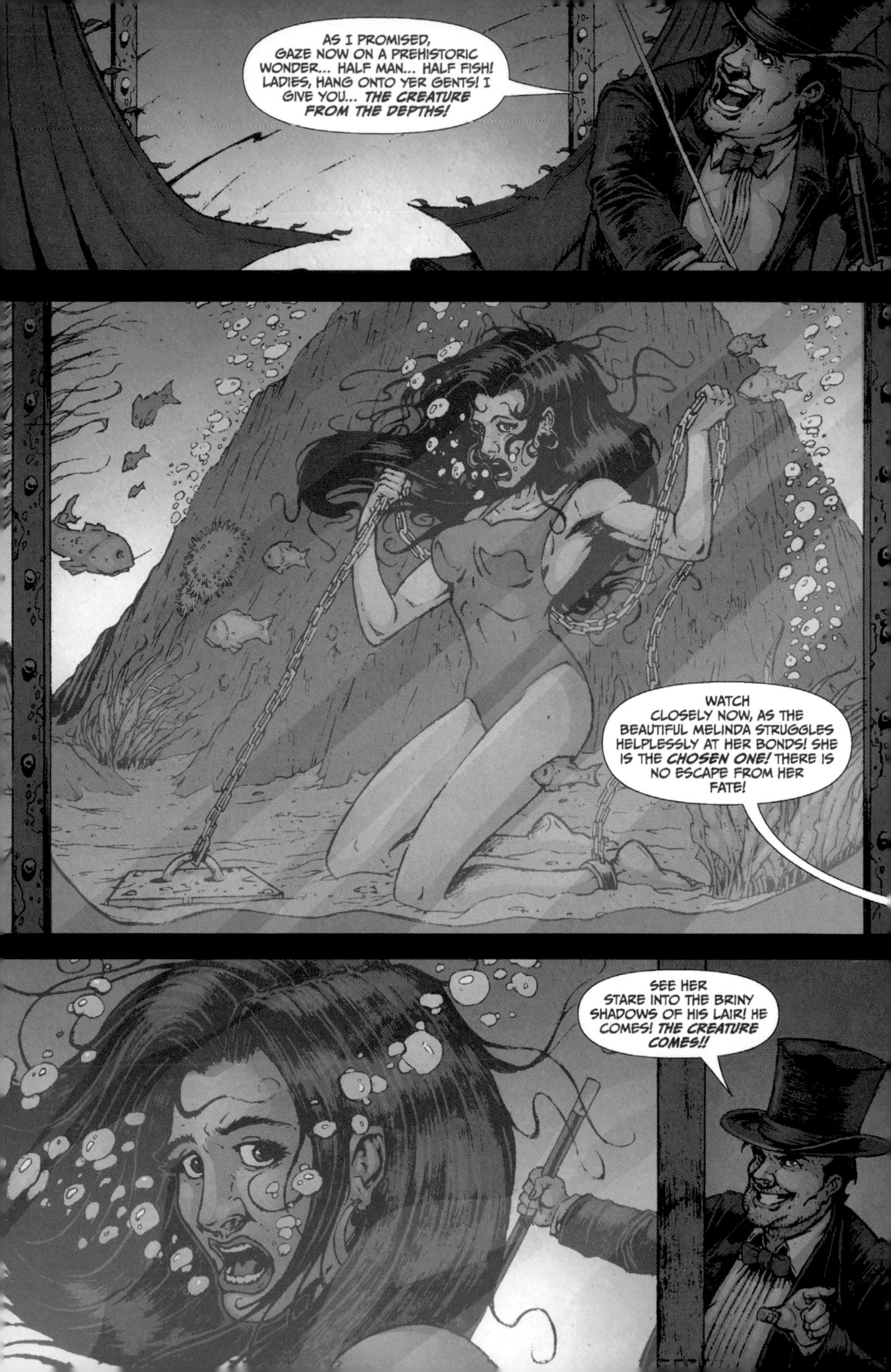
AS I PROMISED, GAZE NOW ON A PREHISTORIC WONDER... HALF MAN... HALF FISH! LADIES, HANG ONTO YER GENTS! I GIVE YOU... *THE CREATURE FROM THE DEPTHS!*
WATCH CLOSELY NOW, AS THE BEAUTIFUL MELINDA STRUGGLES HELPLESSLY AT HER BONDS! SHE IS THE *CHOSEN ONE!* THERE IS NO ESCAPE FROM HER FATE!
SEE HER STARE INTO THE BRINY SHADOWS OF HIS LAIR! HE COMES! *THE CREATURE COMES!!*

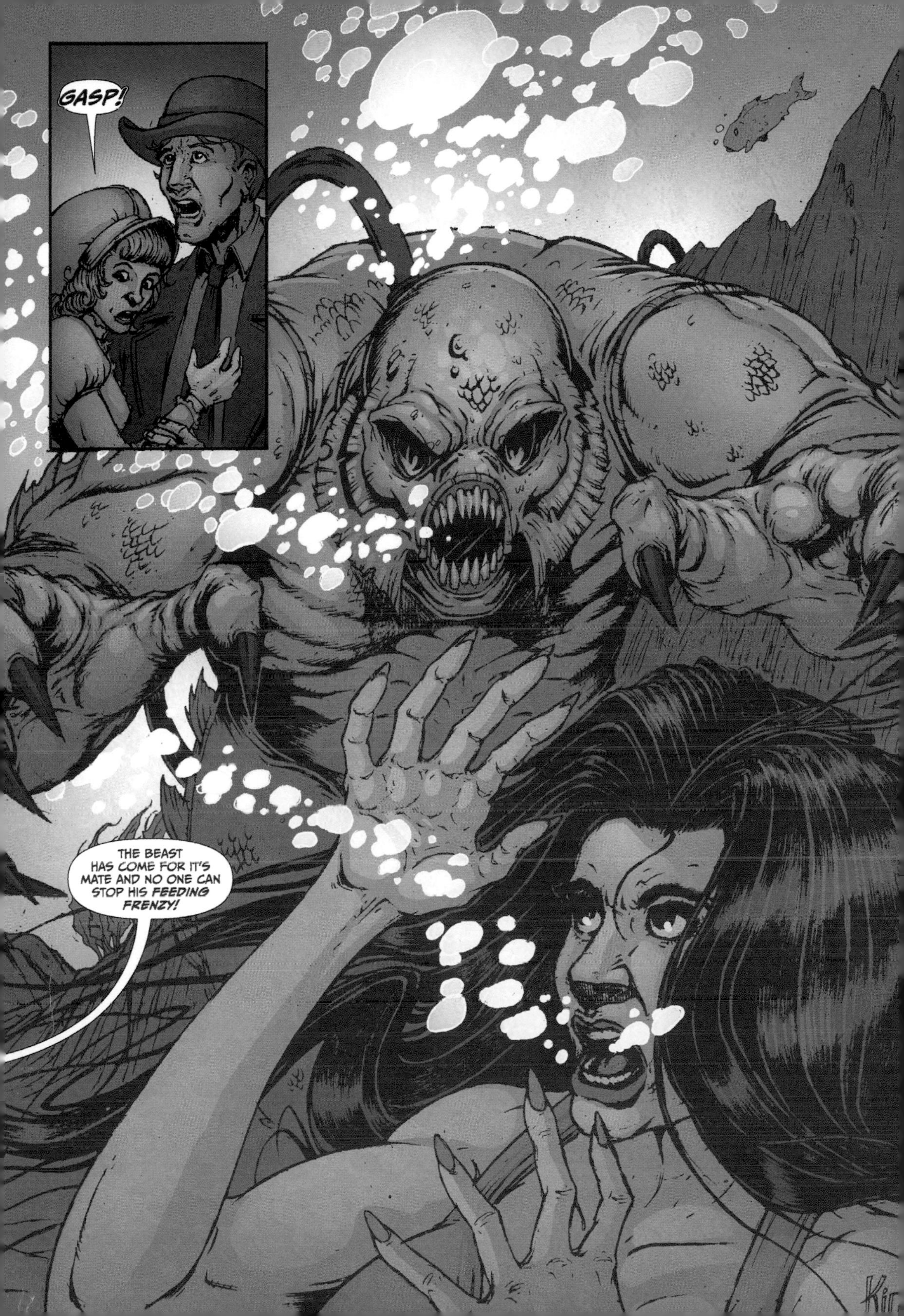
GASP!
THE BEAST HAS COME FOR IT'S MATE AND NO ONE CAN STOP HIS FEEDING FRENZY!

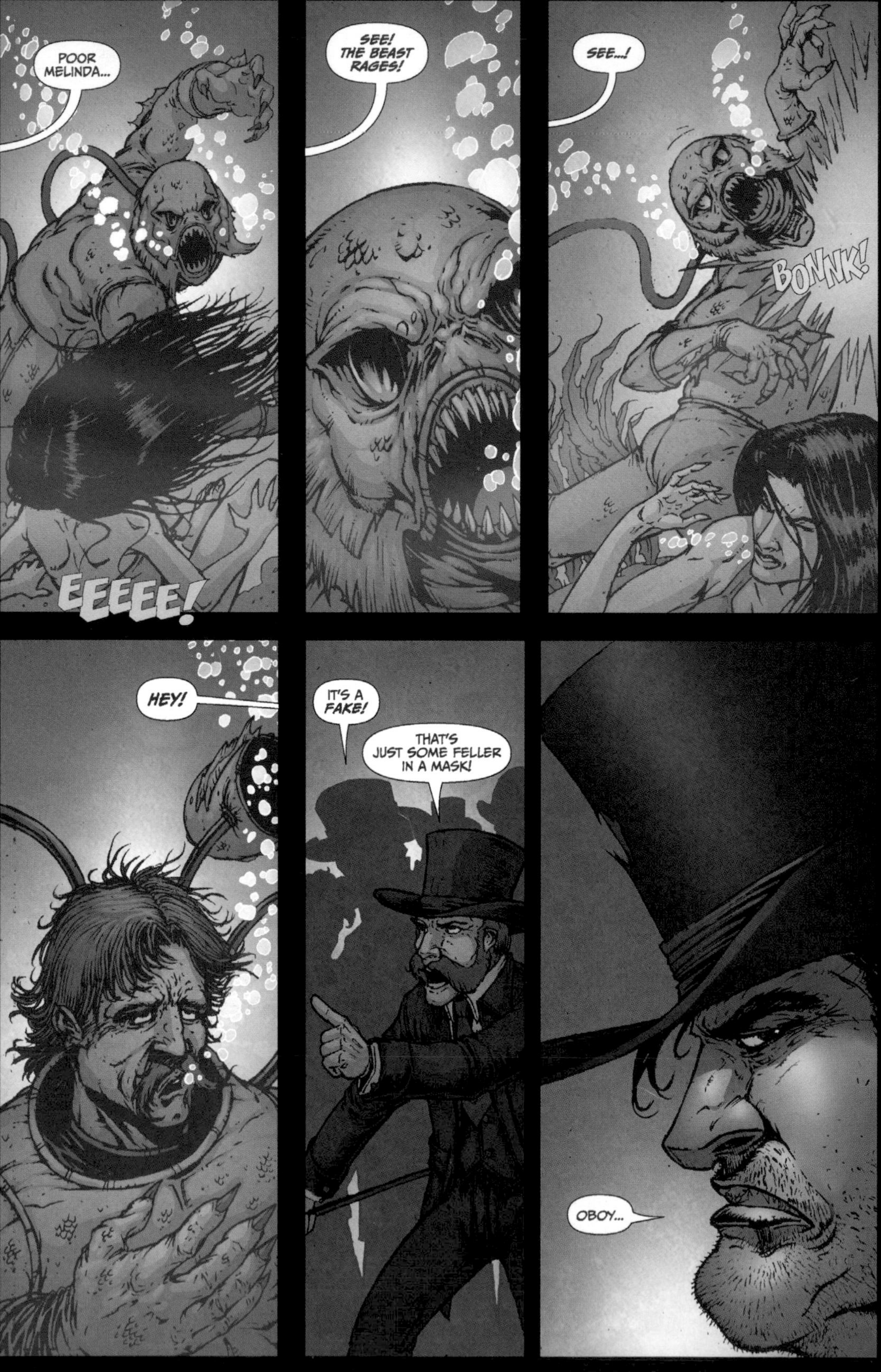
POOR MELINDA...
EEEEEE!
SEE! THE BEAST RAGES!
SEE...!
BONNK!
HEY!
IT'S A FAKE!
THAT'S JUST SOME FELLER IN A MASK!
OBOY...

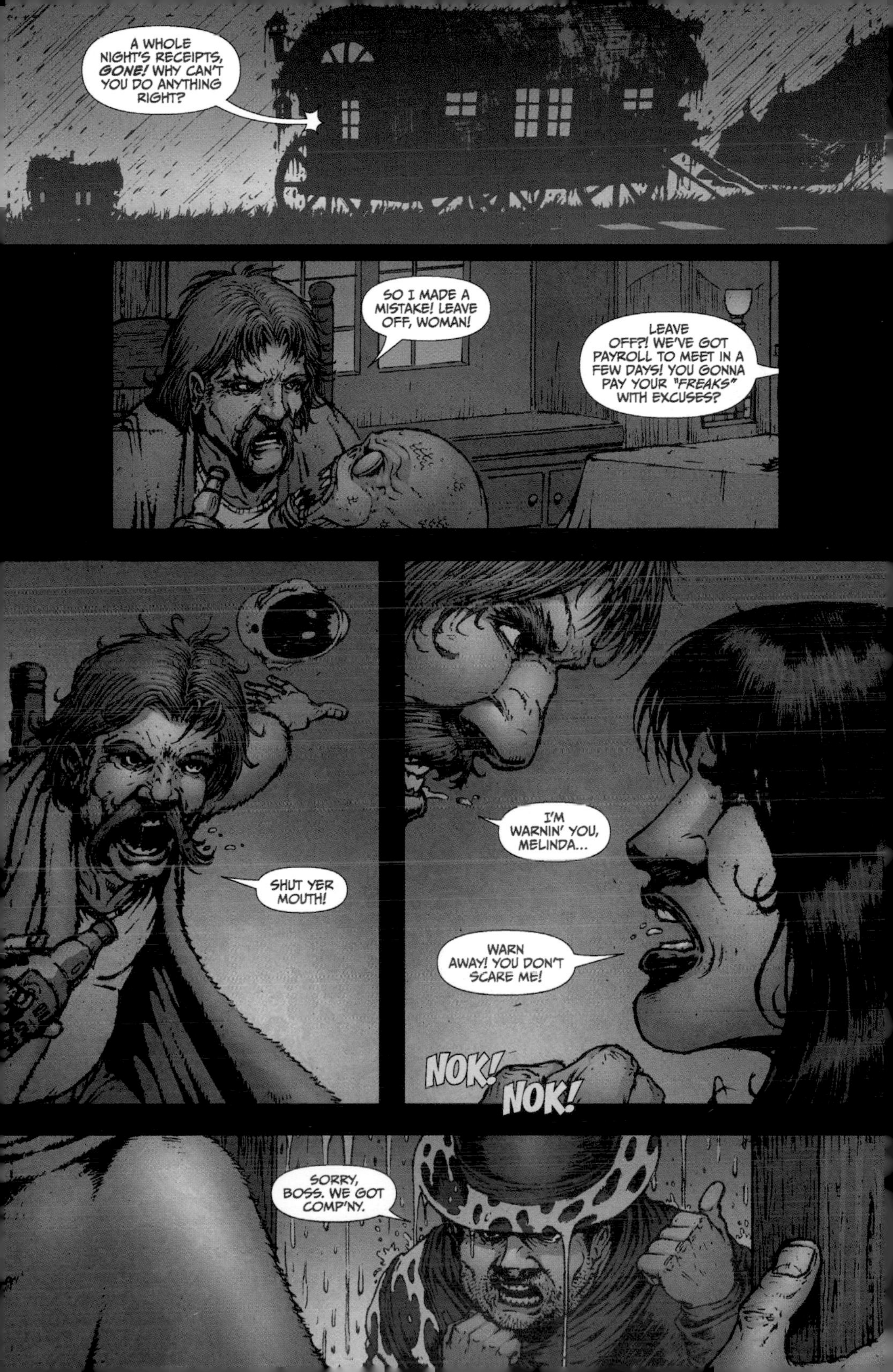
A WHOLE NIGHT'S RECEIPTS, GONE! WHY CAN'T YOU DO ANYTHING RIGHT?
SO I MADE A MISTAKE! LEAVE OFF, WOMAN!
LEAVE OFF?! WE'VE GOT PAYROLL TO MEET IN A FEW DAYS! YOU GONNA PAY YOUR "FREAKS" WITH EXCUSES?
SHUT YER MOUTH!
I'M WARNIN' YOU, MELINDA...
WARN AWAY! YOU DON'T SCARE ME!
NOK!
NOK!
SORRY, BOSS. WE GOT COMP'NY.

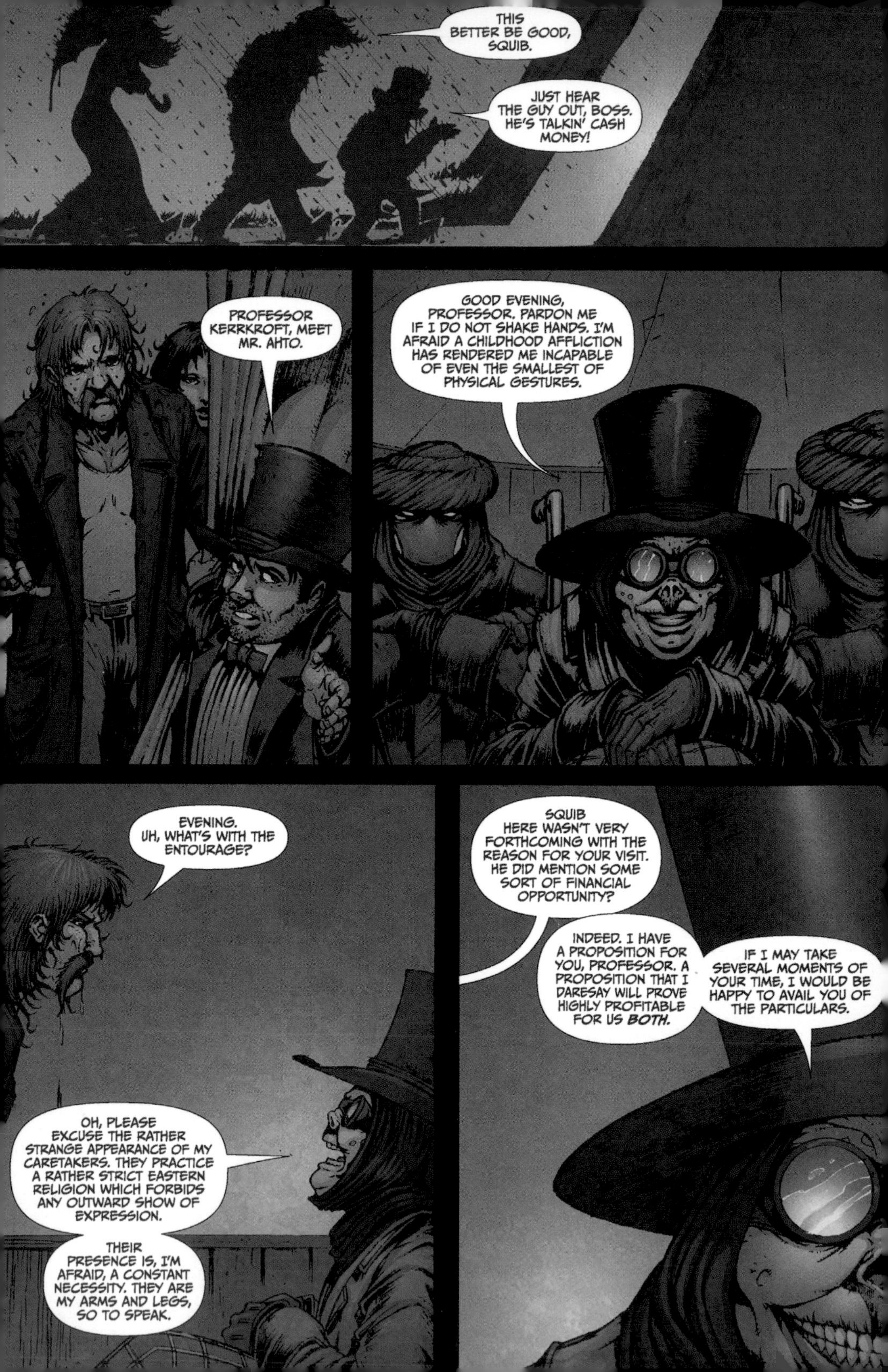
THIS BETTER BE GOOD, SQUIB.
JUST HEAR THE GUY OUT, BOSS. HE'S TALKIN' CASH MONEY!
PROFESSOR KERRKROFT, MEET MR. AHTO.
GOOD EVENING, PROFESSOR. PARDON ME IF I DO NOT SHAKE HANDS. I'M AFRAID A CHILDHOOD AFFLICTION HAS RENDERED ME INCAPABLE OF EVEN THE SMALLEST OF PHYSICAL GESTURES.
EVENING. UH, WHAT'S WITH THE ENTOURAGE?
OH, PLEASE EXCUSE THE RATHER STRANGE APPEARANCE OF MY CARETAKERS. THEY PRACTICE A RATHER STRICT EASTERN RELIGION WHICH FORBIDS ANY OUTWARD SHOW OF EXPRESSION.
THEIR PRESENCE IS, I'M AFRAID, A CONSTANT NECESSITY. THEY ARE MY ARMS AND LEGS, SO TO SPEAK.
SQUIB HERE WASN'T VERY FORTHCOMING WITH THE REASON FOR YOUR VISIT. HE DID MENTION SOME SORT OF FINANCIAL OPPORTUNITY?
INDEED. I HAVE A PROPOSITION FOR YOU, PROFESSOR. A PROPOSITION THAT I DARESAY WILL PROVE HIGHLY PROFITABLE FOR US *BOTH.*
IF I MAY TAKE SEVERAL MOMENTS OF YOUR TIME, I WOULD BE HAPPY TO AVAIL YOU OF THE PARTICULARS.

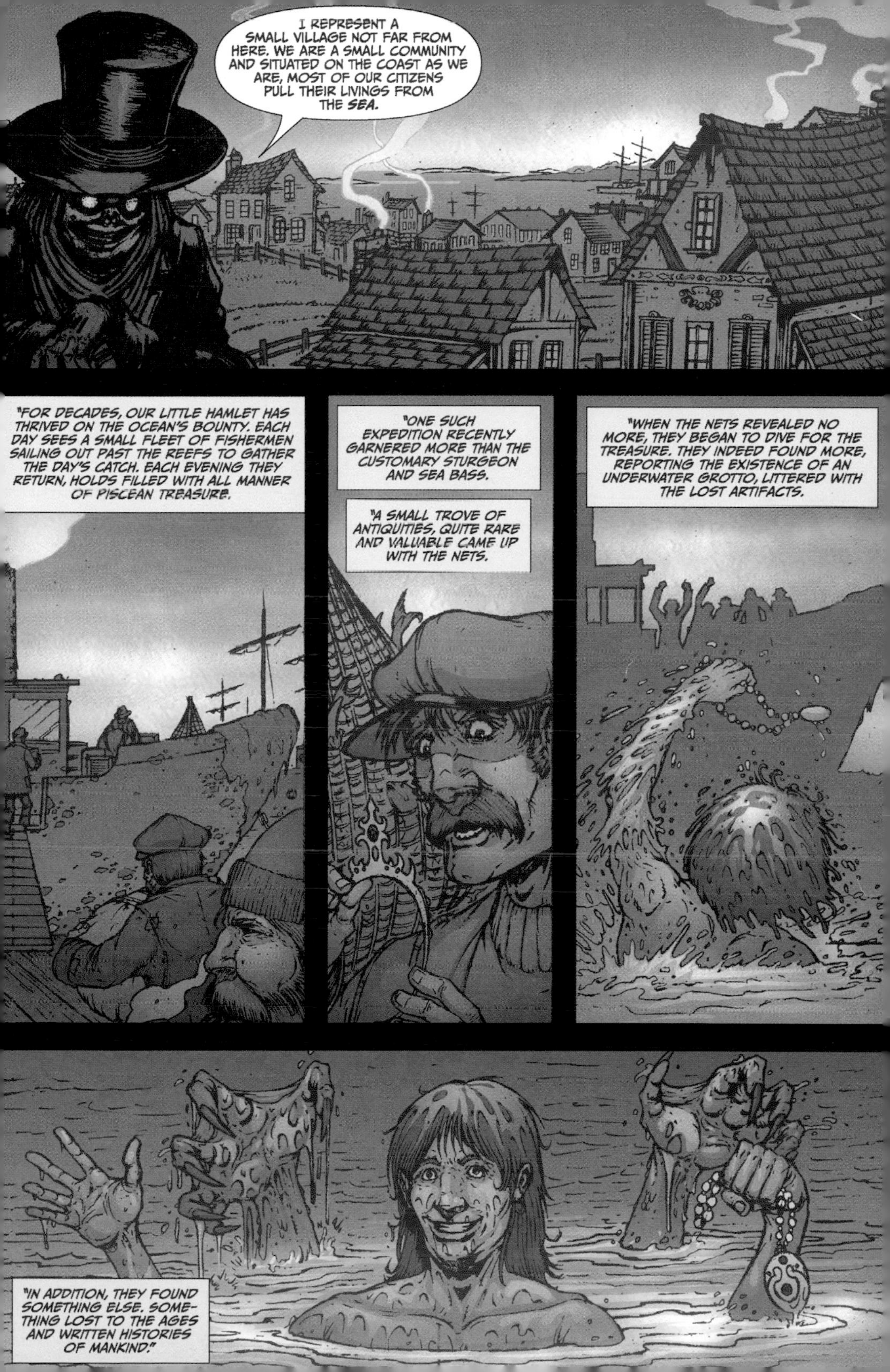
I REPRESENT A SMALL VILLAGE NOT FAR FROM HERE. WE ARE A SMALL COMMUNITY AND SITUATED ON THE COAST AS WE ARE, MOST OF OUR CITIZENS PULL THEIR LIVINGS FROM THE SEA.
"FOR DECADES, OUR LITTLE HAMLET HAS THRIVED ON THE OCEAN'S BOUNTY. EACH DAY SEES A SMALL FLEET OF FISHERMEN SAILING OUT PAST THE REEFS TO GATHER THE DAY'S CATCH. EACH EVENING THEY RETURN, HOLDS FILLED WITH ALL MANNER OF PISCEAN TREASURE.
"ONE SUCH EXPEDITION RECENTLY GARNERED MORE THAN THE CUSTOMARY STURGEON AND SEA BASS.
"A SMALL TROVE OF ANTIQUITIES, QUITE RARE AND VALUABLE CAME UP WITH THE NETS.
"WHEN THE NETS REVEALED NO MORE, THEY BEGAN TO DIVE FOR THE TREASURE. THEY INDEED FOUND MORE, REPORTING THE EXISTENCE OF AN UNDERWATER GROTTO, LITTERED WITH THE LOST ARTIFACTS.
"IN ADDITION, THEY FOUND SOMETHING ELSE. SOME-THING LOST TO THE AGES AND WRITTEN HISTORIES OF MANKIND."

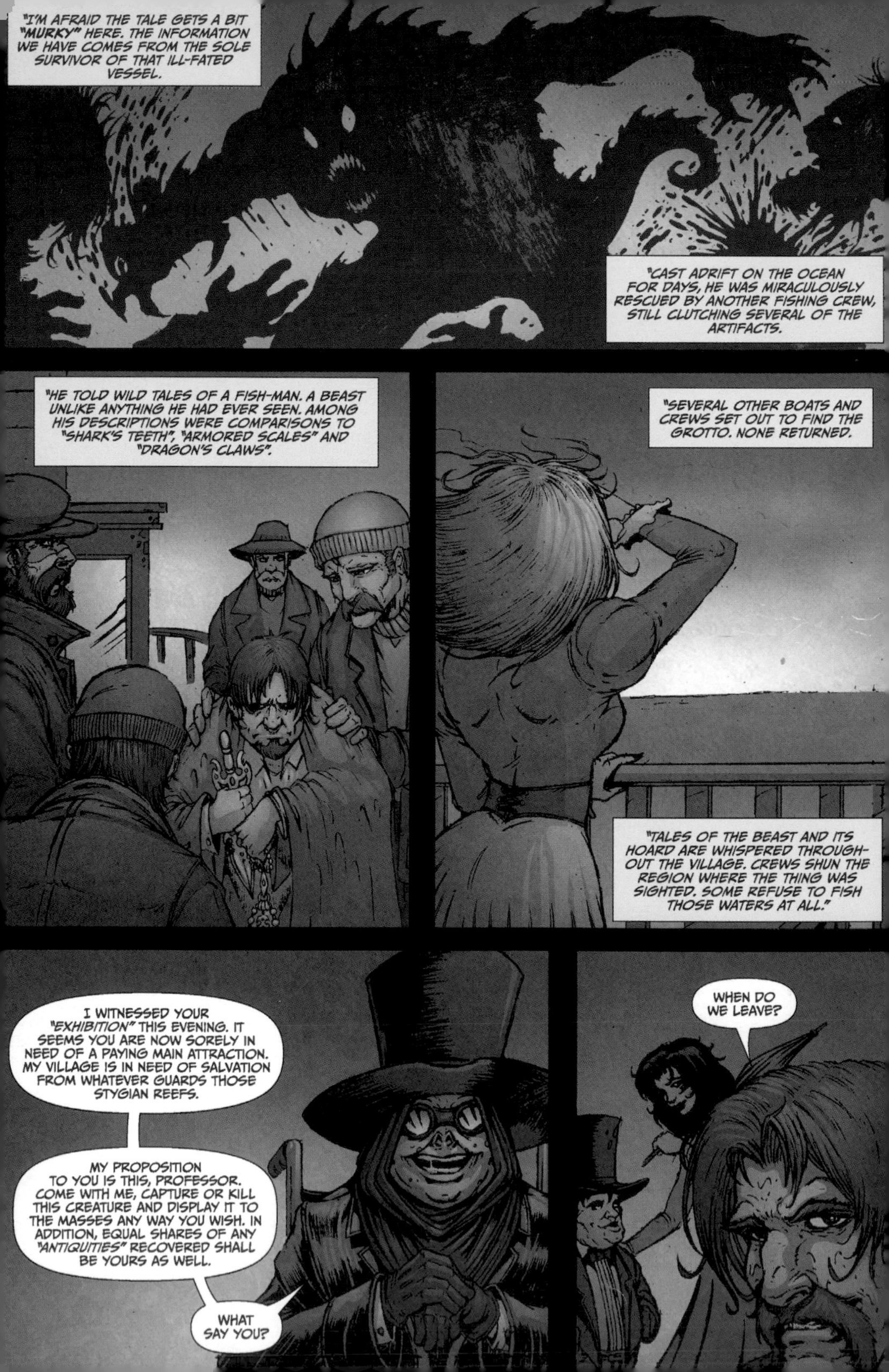
"I'M AFRAID THE TALE GETS A BIT "MURKY" HERE. THE INFORMATION WE HAVE COMES FROM THE SOLE SURVIVOR OF THAT ILL-FATED VESSEL.
"CAST ADRIFT ON THE OCEAN FOR DAYS, HE WAS MIRACULOUSLY RESCUED BY ANOTHER FISHING CREW, STILL CLUTCHING SEVERAL OF THE ARTIFACTS.
"HE TOLD WILD TALES OF A FISH-MAN. A BEAST UNLIKE ANYTHING HE HAD EVER SEEN. AMONG HIS DESCRIPTIONS WERE COMPARISONS TO "SHARK'S TEETH", "ARMORED SCALES" AND "DRAGON'S CLAWS".
"SEVERAL OTHER BOATS AND CREWS SET OUT TO FIND THE GROTTO. NONE RETURNED.
"TALES OF THE BEAST AND ITS HOARD ARE WHISPERED THROUGH-OUT THE VILLAGE. CREWS SHUN THE REGION WHERE THE THING WAS SIGHTED. SOME REFUSE TO FISH THOSE WATERS AT ALL."
I WITNESSED YOUR "EXHIBITION" THIS EVENING. IT SEEMS YOU ARE NOW SORELY IN NEED OF A PAYING MAIN ATTRACTION. MY VILLAGE IS IN NEED OF SALVATION FROM WHATEVER GUARDS THOSE STYGIAN REEFS.
MY PROPOSITION TO YOU IS THIS, PROFESSOR. COME WITH ME, CAPTURE OR KILL THIS CREATURE AND DISPLAY IT TO THE MASSES ANY WAY YOU WISH. IN ADDITION, EQUAL SHARES OF ANY "ANTIQUITIES" RECOVERED SHALL BE YOURS AS WELL.
WHAT SAY YOU?
WHEN DO WE LEAVE?

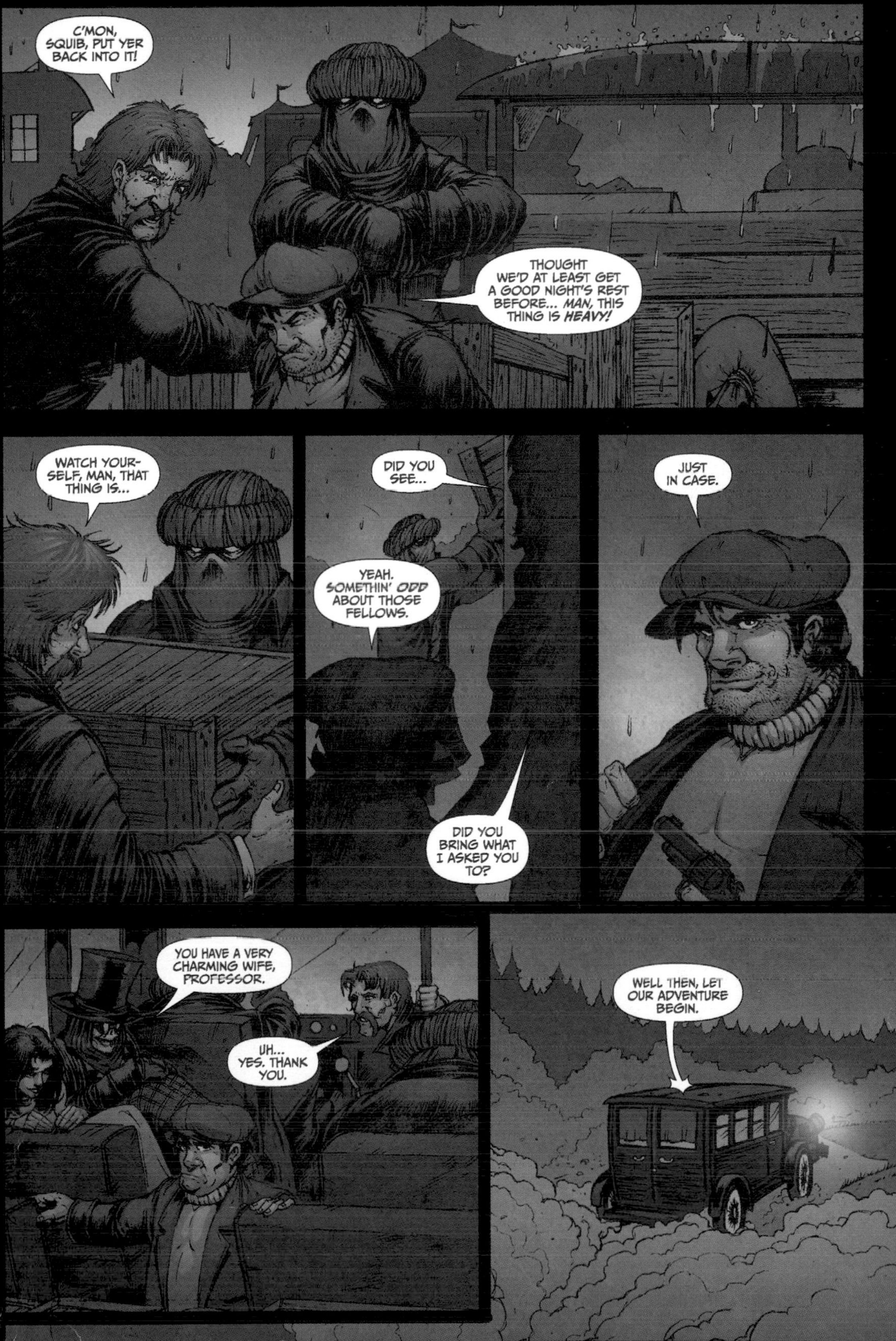
C'MON, SQUIB, PUT YER BACK INTO IT!
THOUGHT WE'D AT LEAST GET A GOOD NIGHT'S REST BEFORE... MAN, THIS THING IS HEAVY!
WATCH YOURSELF, MAN, THAT THING IS...
DID YOU SEE...
YEAH. SOMETHIN' ODD ABOUT THOSE FELLOWS.
DID YOU BRING WHAT I ASKED YOU TO?
JUST IN CASE.
YOU HAVE A VERY CHARMING WIFE, PROFESSOR.
UH... YES. THANK YOU.
WELL THEN, LET OUR ADVENTURE BEGIN.

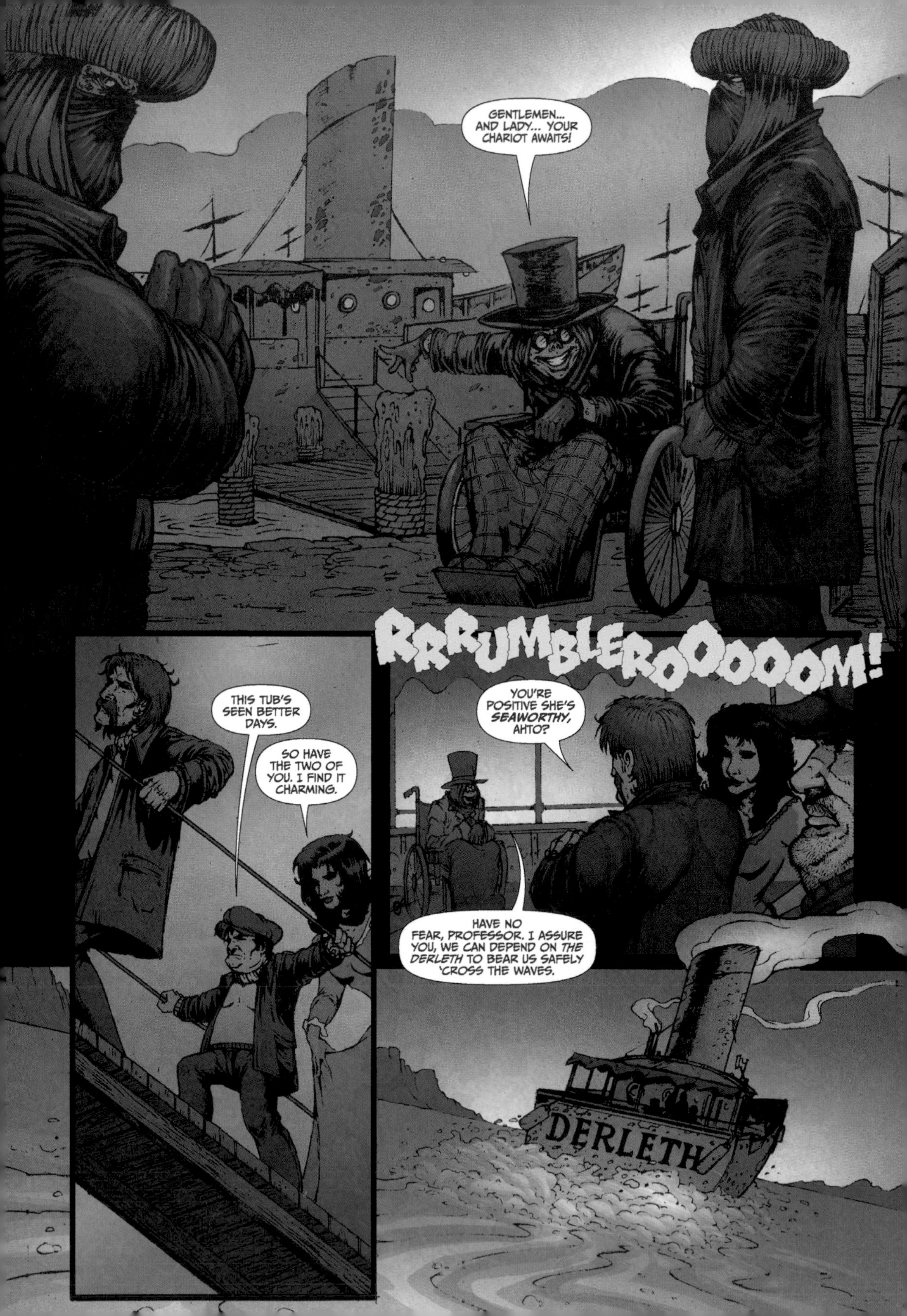
GENTLEMEN... AND LADY... YOUR CHARIOT AWAITS!
THIS TUB'S SEEN BETTER DAYS.
SO HAVE THE TWO OF YOU. I FIND IT CHARMING.
RRRUMBLEROOOOOM!
YOU'RE POSITIVE SHE'S SEAWORTHY, AHTO?
HAVE NO FEAR, PROFESSOR. I ASSURE YOU, WE CAN DEPEND ON THE DERLETH TO BEAR US SAFELY 'CROSS THE WAVES.
DERLETH

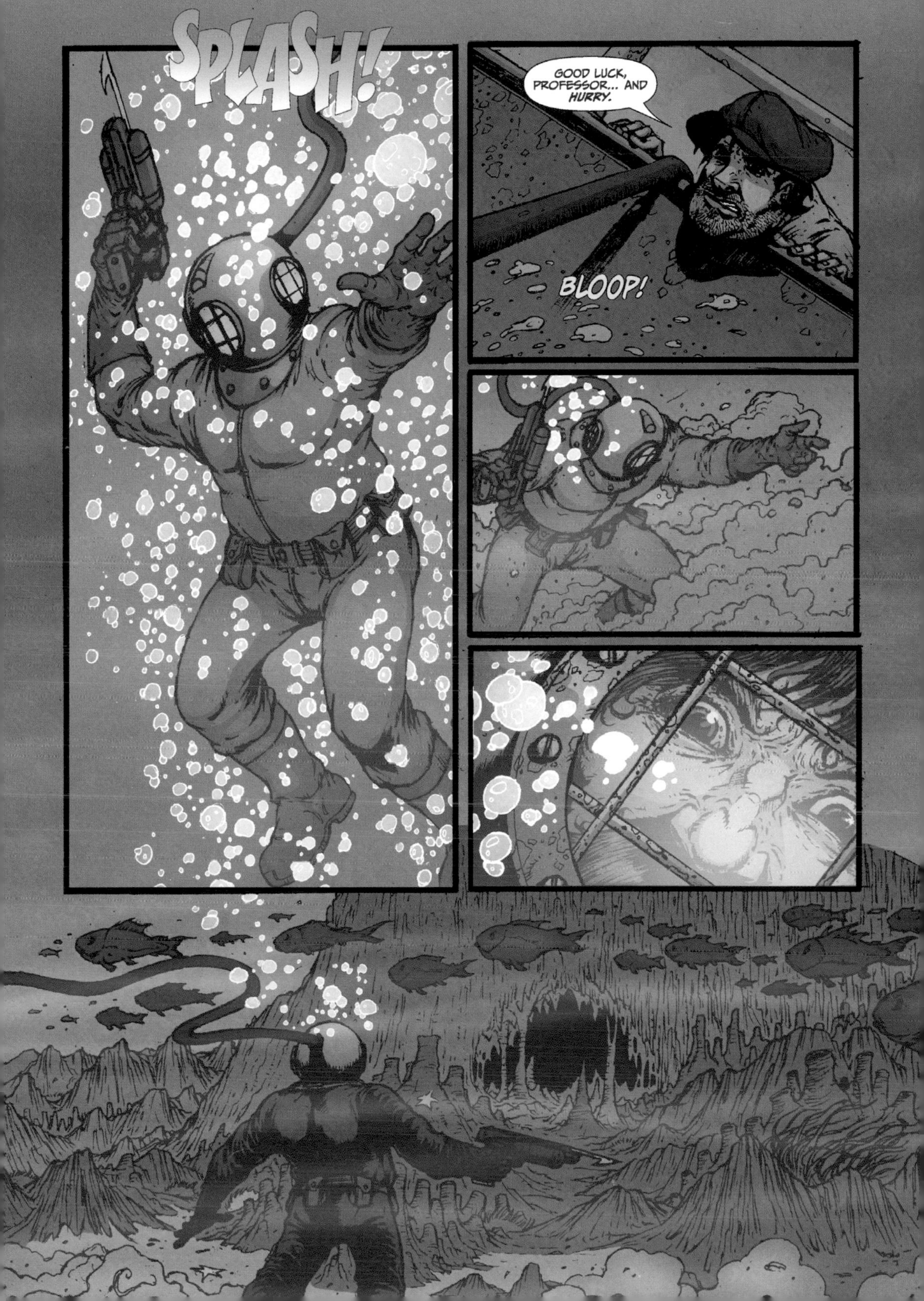
SPLASH!!
GOOD LUCK, PROFESSOR... AND HURRY.
BLOOP!

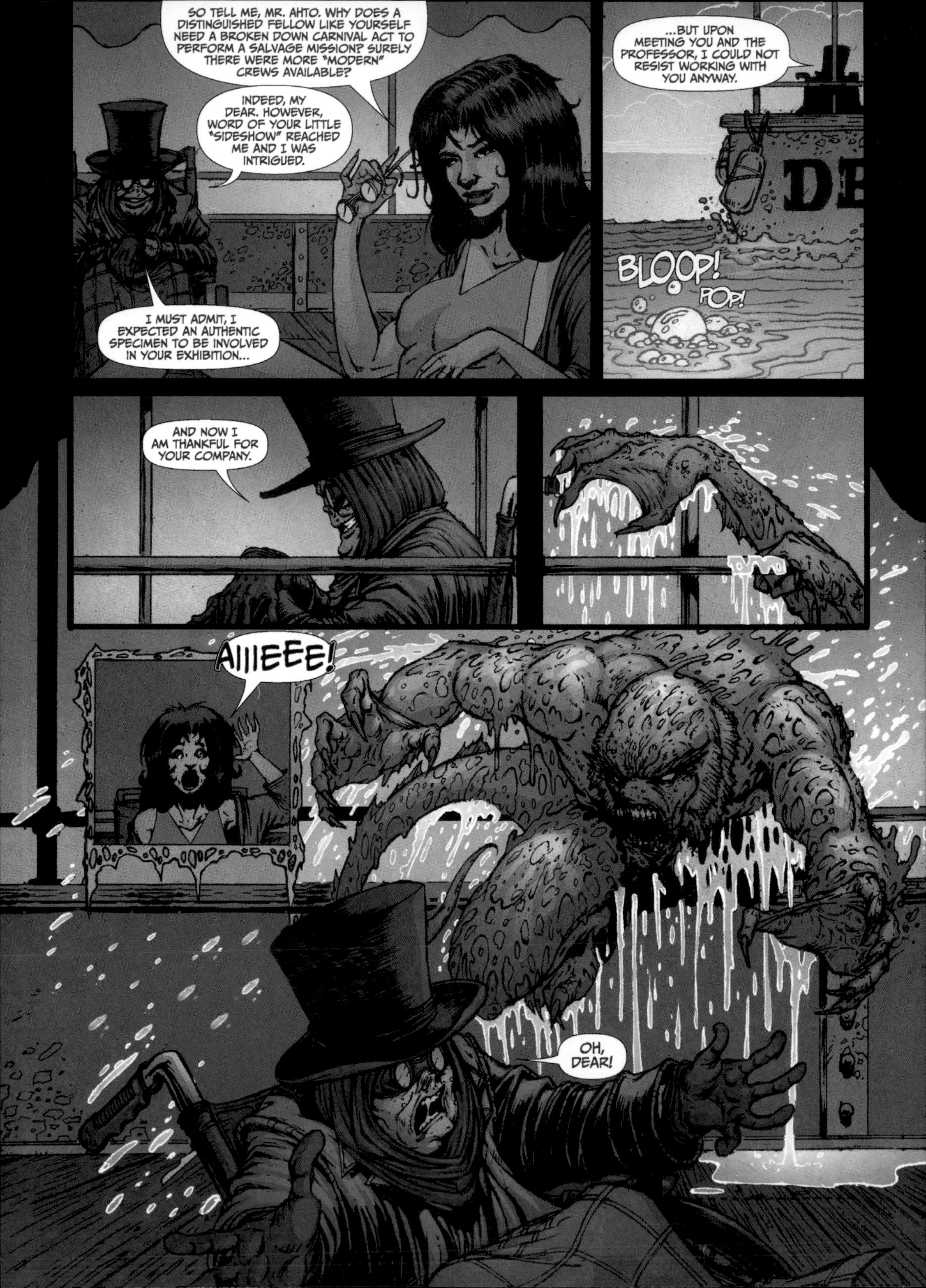
SO TELL ME, MR. AHTO. WHY DOES A DISTINGUISHED FELLOW LIKE YOURSELF NEED A BROKEN DOWN CARNIVAL ACT TO PERFORM A SALVAGE MISSION? SURELY THERE WERE MORE "MODERN" CREWS AVAILABLE?
INDEED, MY DEAR. HOWEVER, WORD OF YOUR LITTLE "SIDESHOW" REACHED ME AND I WAS INTRIGUED.
I MUST ADMIT, I EXPECTED AN AUTHENTIC SPECIMEN TO BE INVOLVED IN YOUR EXHIBITION...
...BUT UPON MEETING YOU AND THE PROFESSOR, I COULD NOT RESIST WORKING WITH YOU ANYWAY.
BLOOP!
POP!
AND NOW I AM THANKFUL FOR YOUR COMPANY.
AIIIEEE!
OH, DEAR!

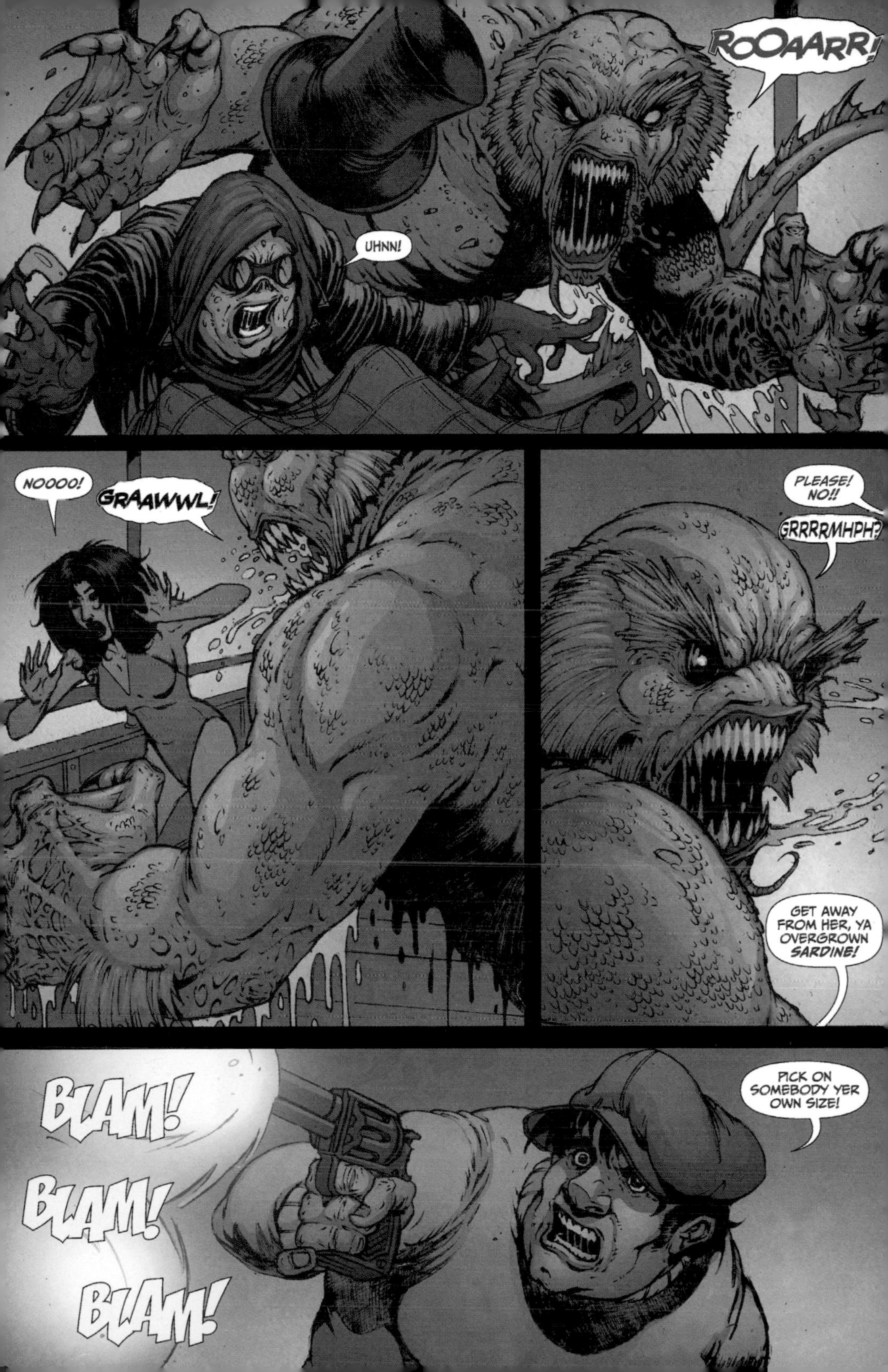
ROOAARR!
UHNN!
NOOOO!
GRAAWWL!
PLEASE! NO!!
GRRRRMHPH?
GET AWAY FROM HER, YA OVERGROWN SARDINE!
BLAM!
BLAM!
BLAM!
PICK ON SOMEBODY YER OWN SIZE!

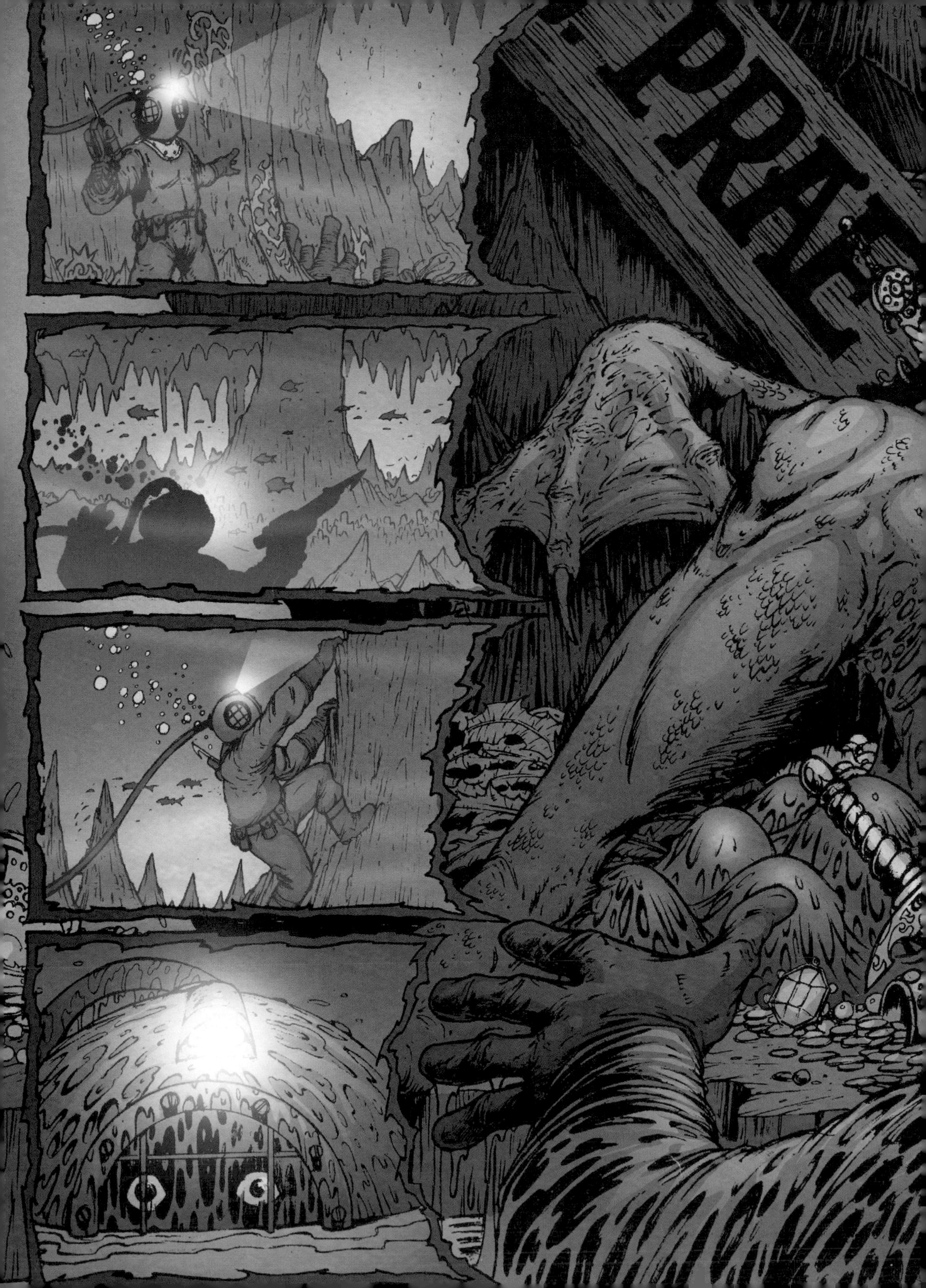

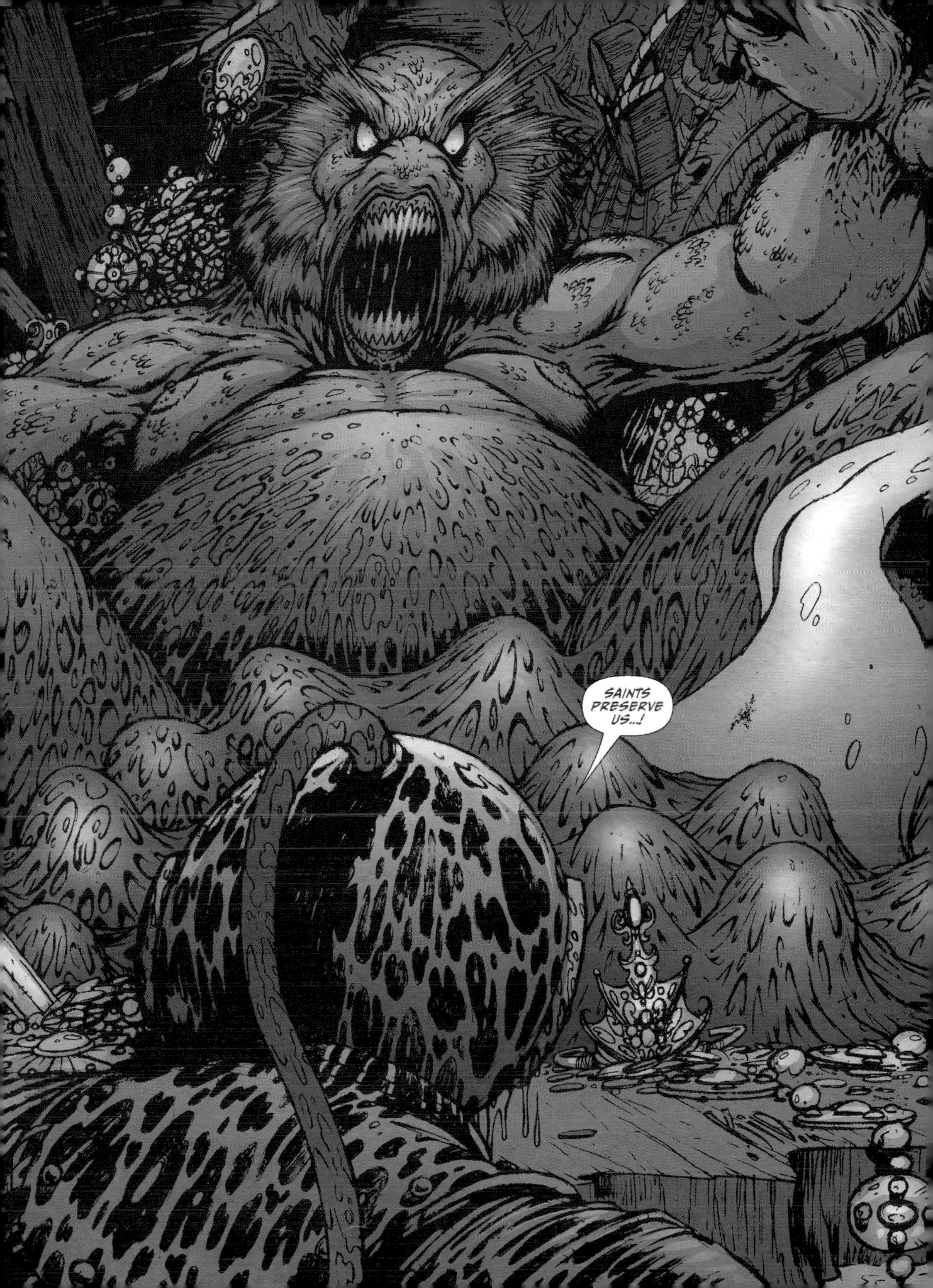
SAINTS PRESERVE US...!

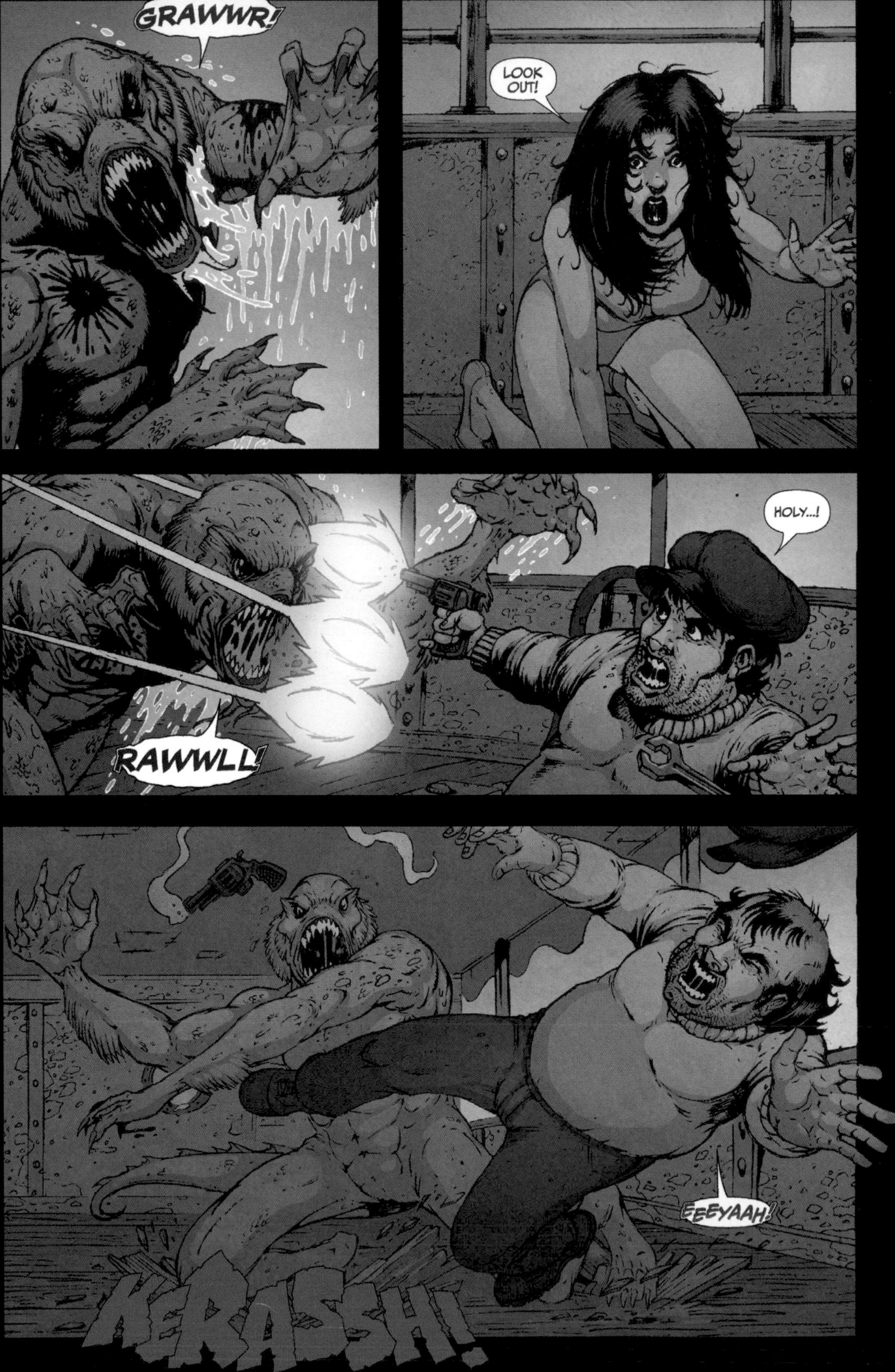
GRAWWR!
LOOK OUT!
HOLY...!
RAWWLL!
EEEYAAH!
KERASSH!!

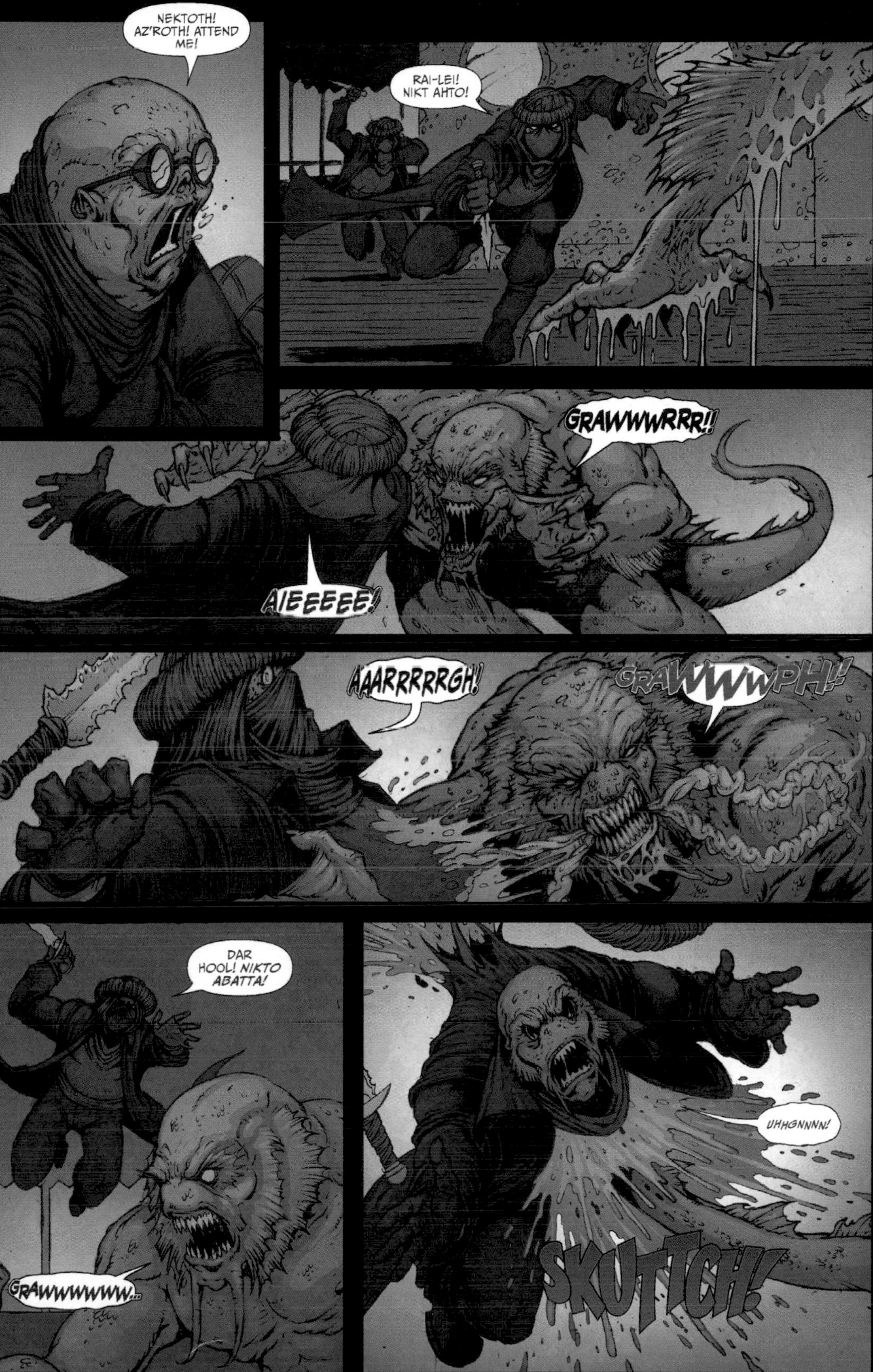
NEKTOTH! AZ'ROTH! ATTEND ME!
RAI-LEI! NIKT AHTO!
GRAWWWRRR!!
AIEEEEEE!
AAARRRRRGH!
GRAWWWPH!!
DAR HOOL! NIKTO ABATTA!
GRAWWWWWW...
UHHGNNNN!
SKUTTCH!

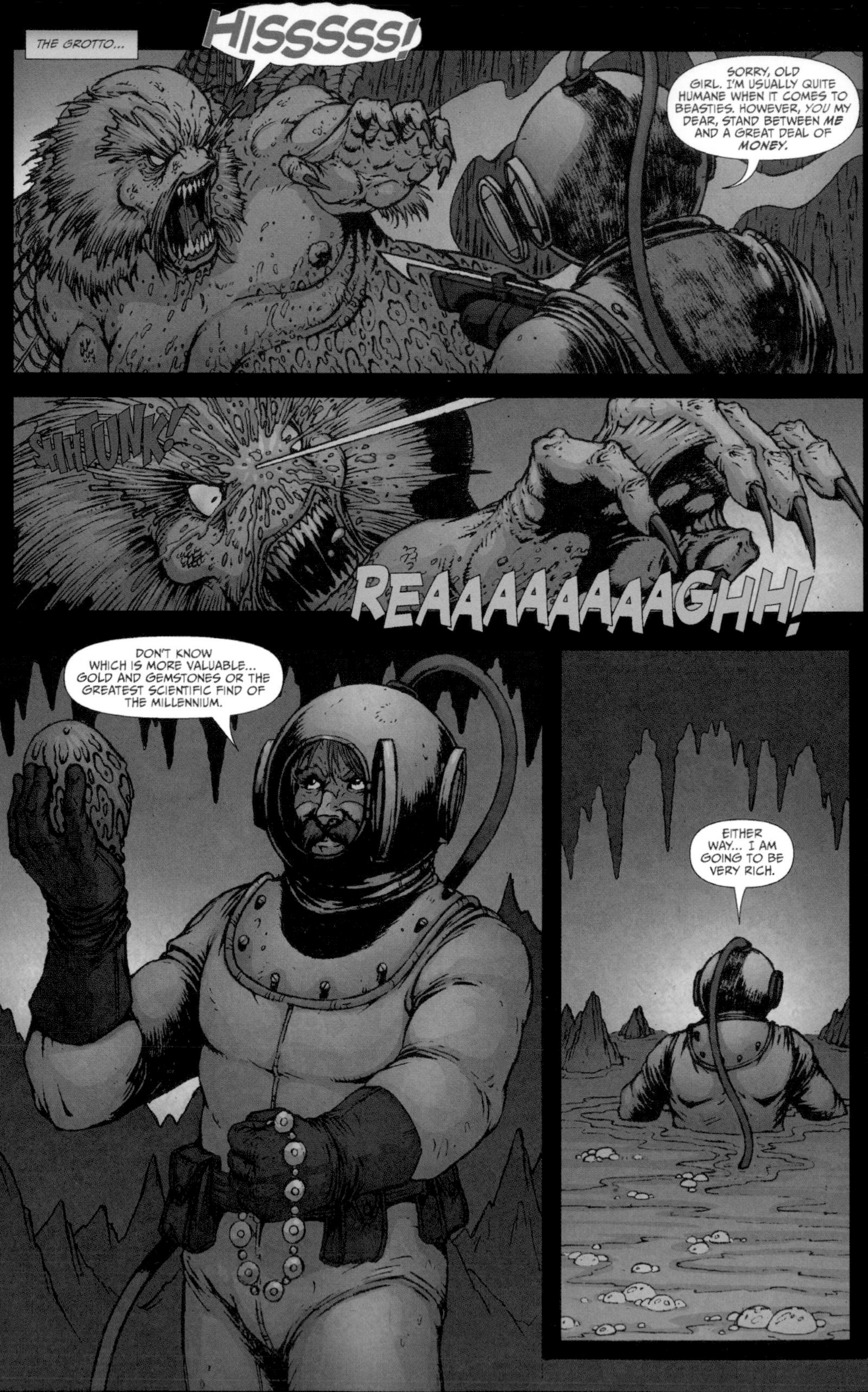
THE GROTTO...
HISSSSS!
SORRY, OLD GIRL. I'M USUALLY QUITE HUMANE WHEN IT COMES TO BEASTIES. HOWEVER, YOU MY DEAR, STAND BETWEEN ME AND A GREAT DEAL OF MONEY.
SHHTUNK!
REAAAAAAAAGHH!
DON'T KNOW WHICH IS MORE VALUABLE... GOLD AND GEMSTONES OR THE GREATEST SCIENTIFIC FIND OF THE MILLENNIUM.
EITHER WAY... I AM GOING TO BE VERY RICH.

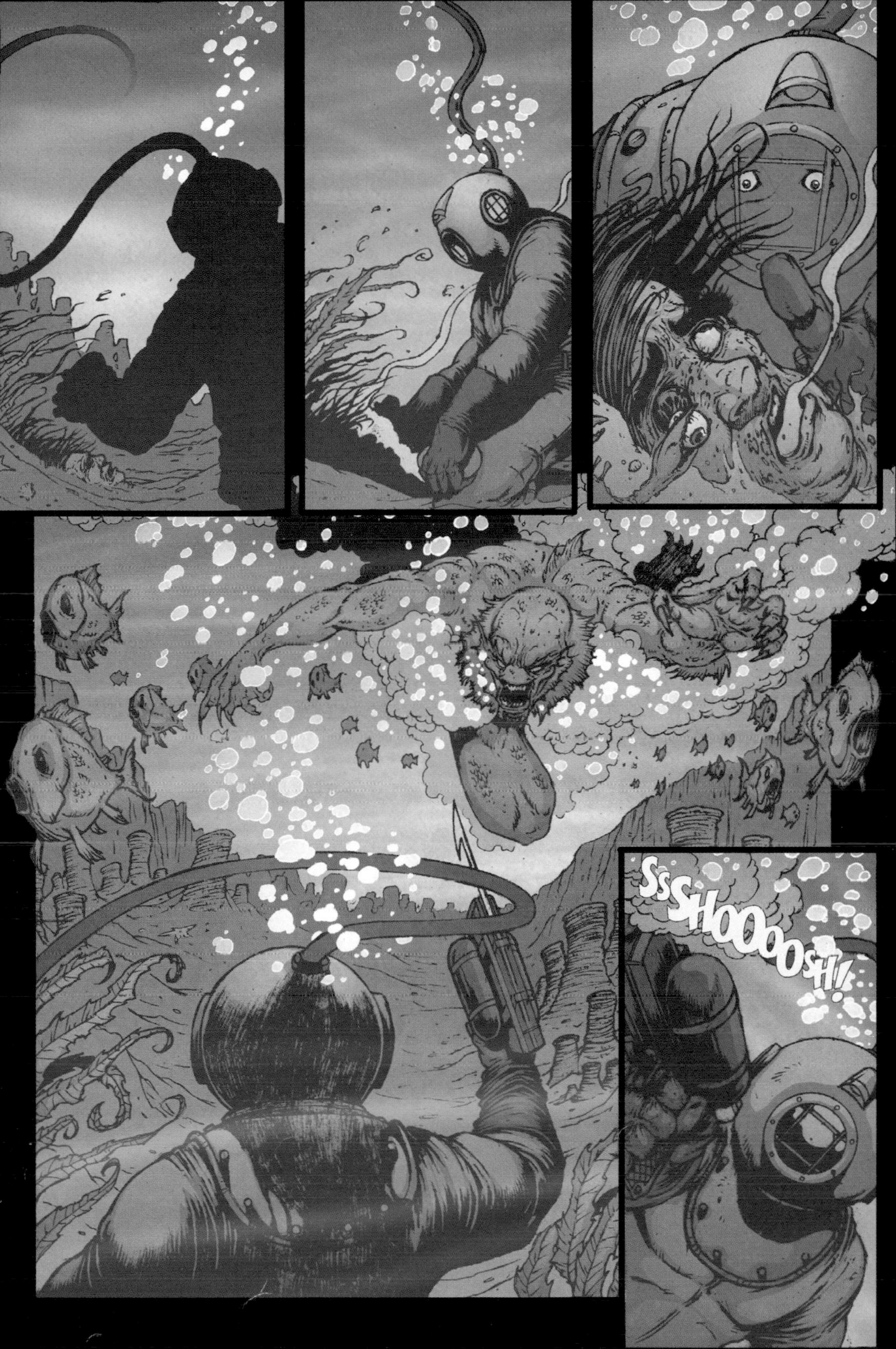
SsSHOOOOOSH!!

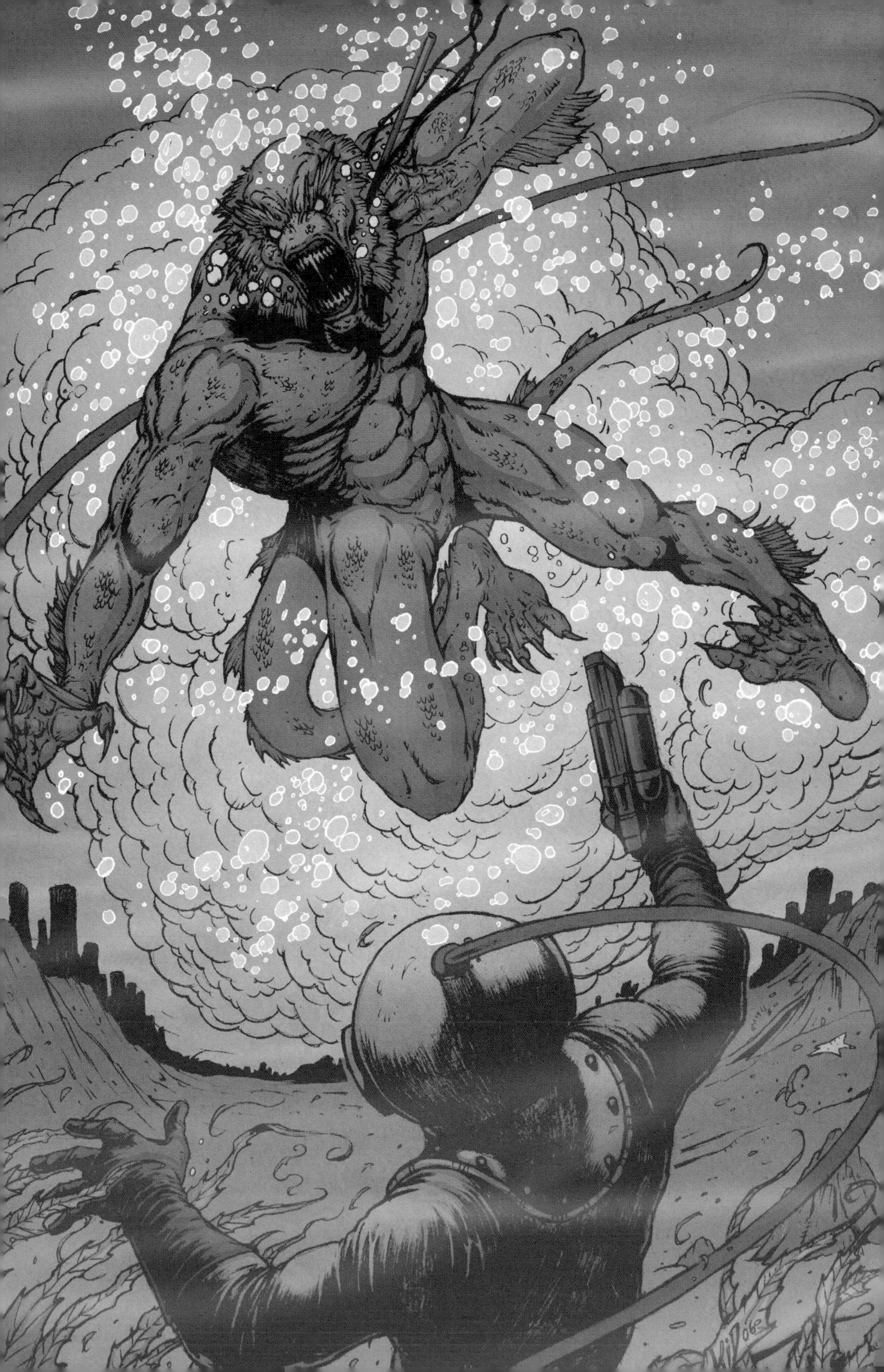

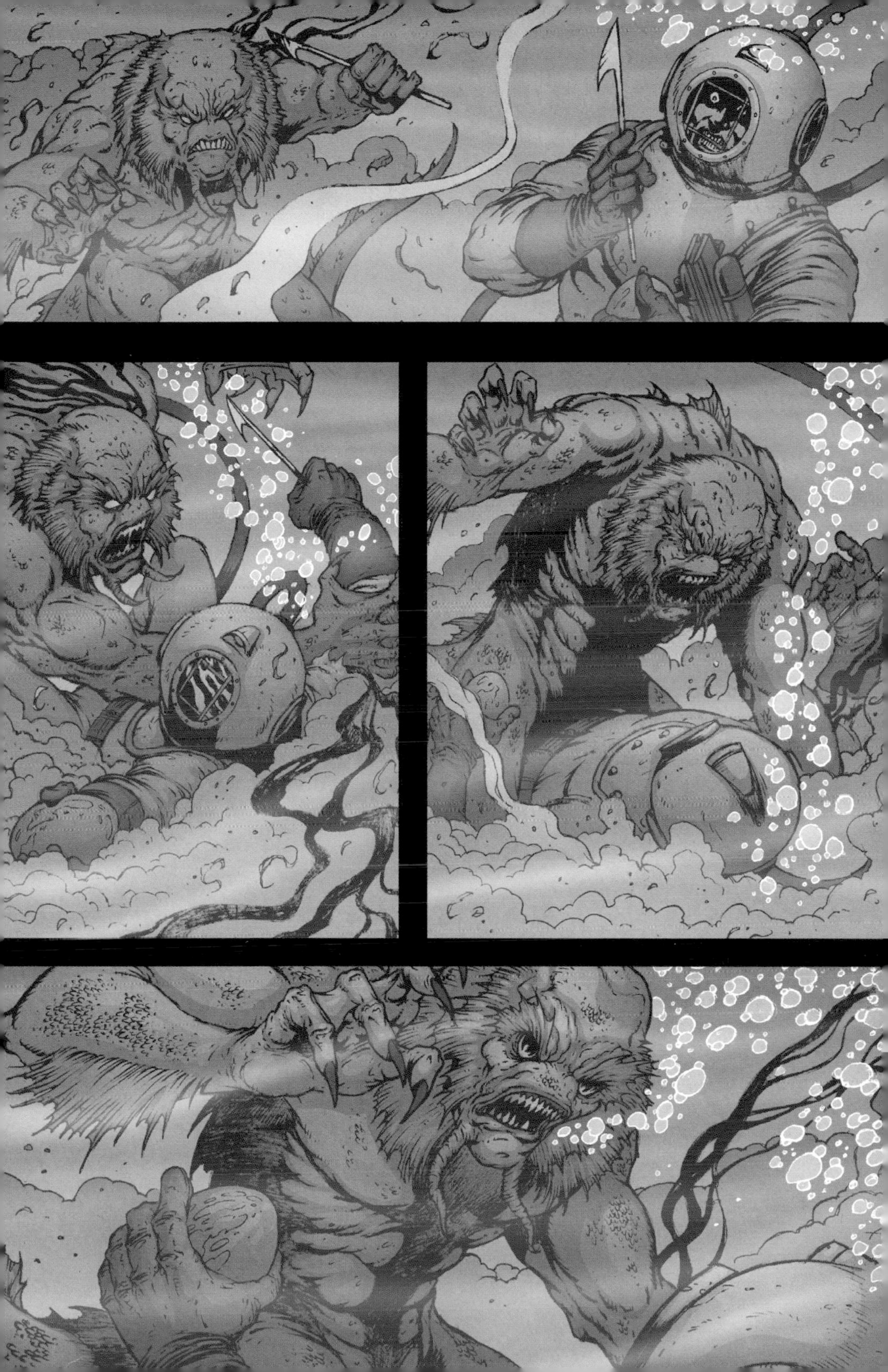

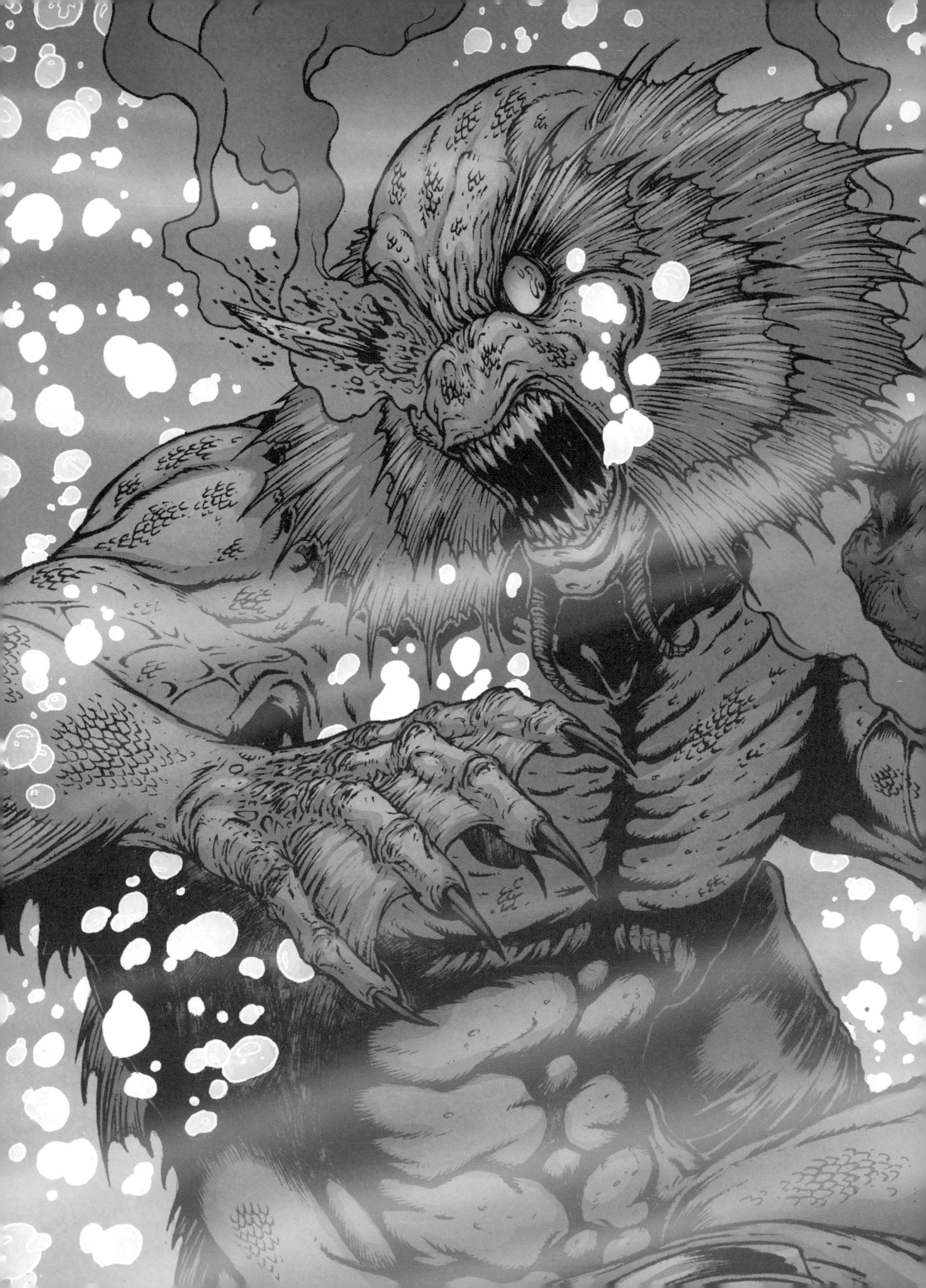

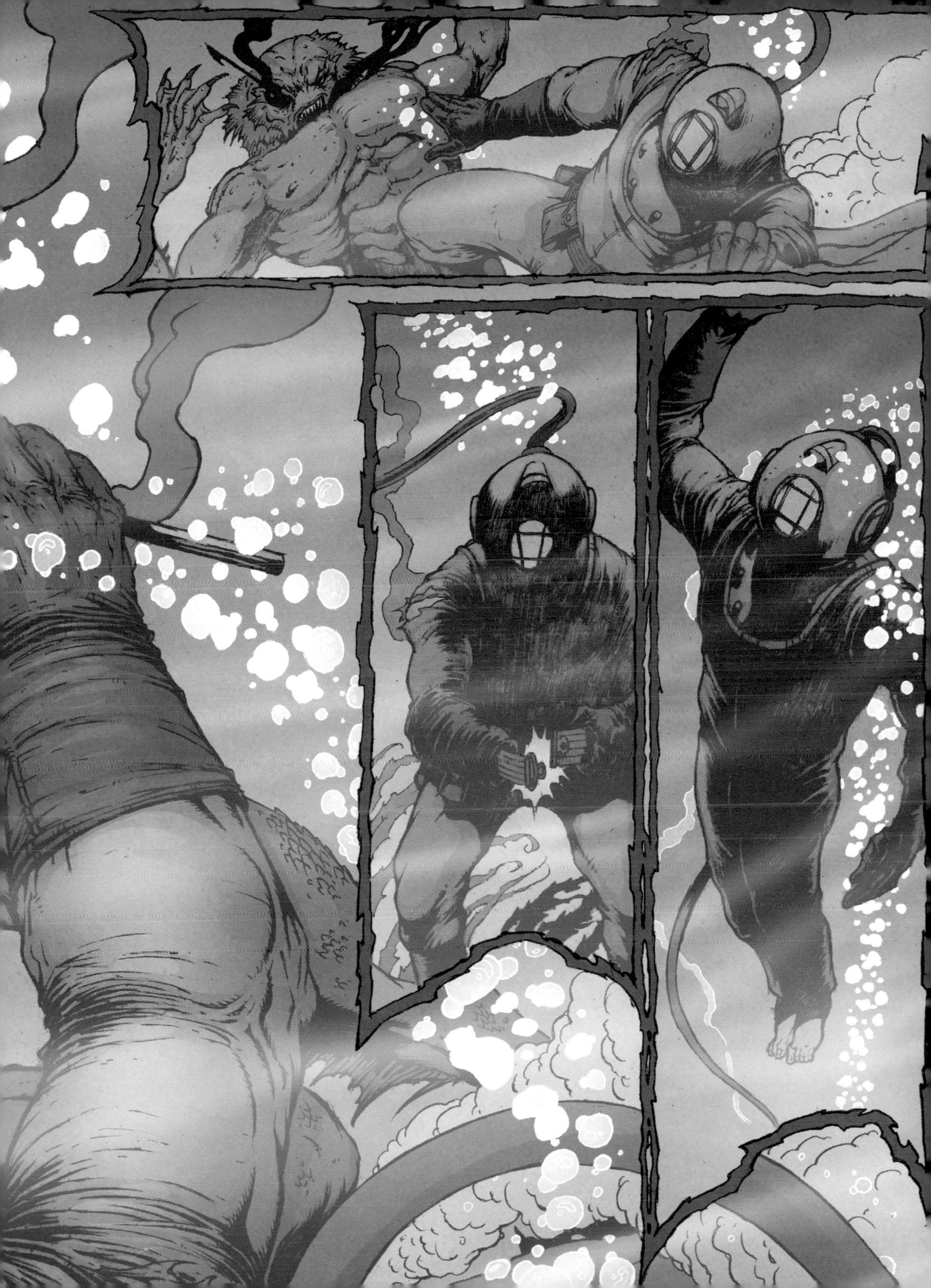

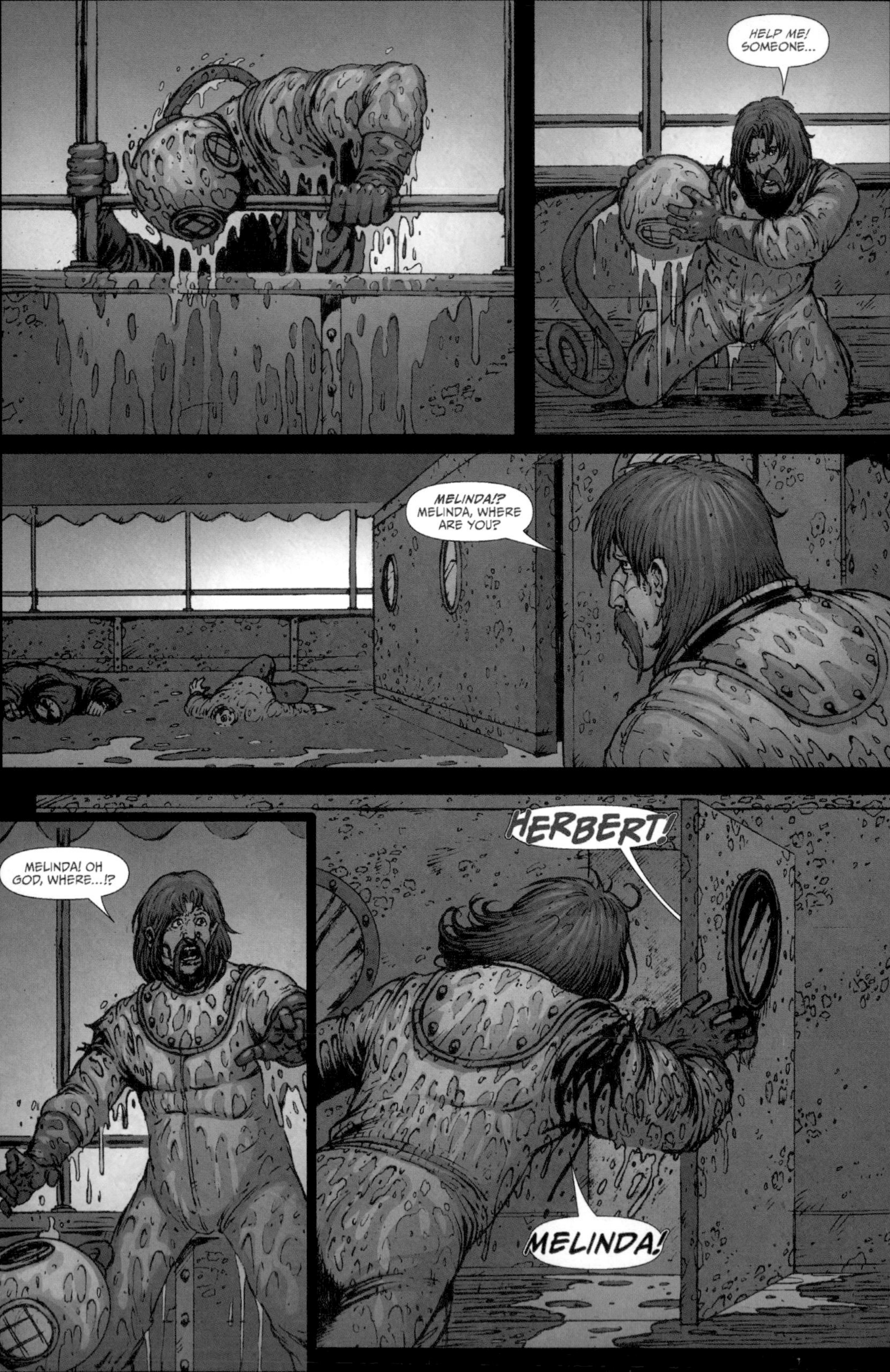
HELP ME! SOMEONE...
MELINDA!? MELINDA, WHERE ARE YOU?
MELINDA! OH GOD, WHERE...!?
HERBERT!
MELINDA!

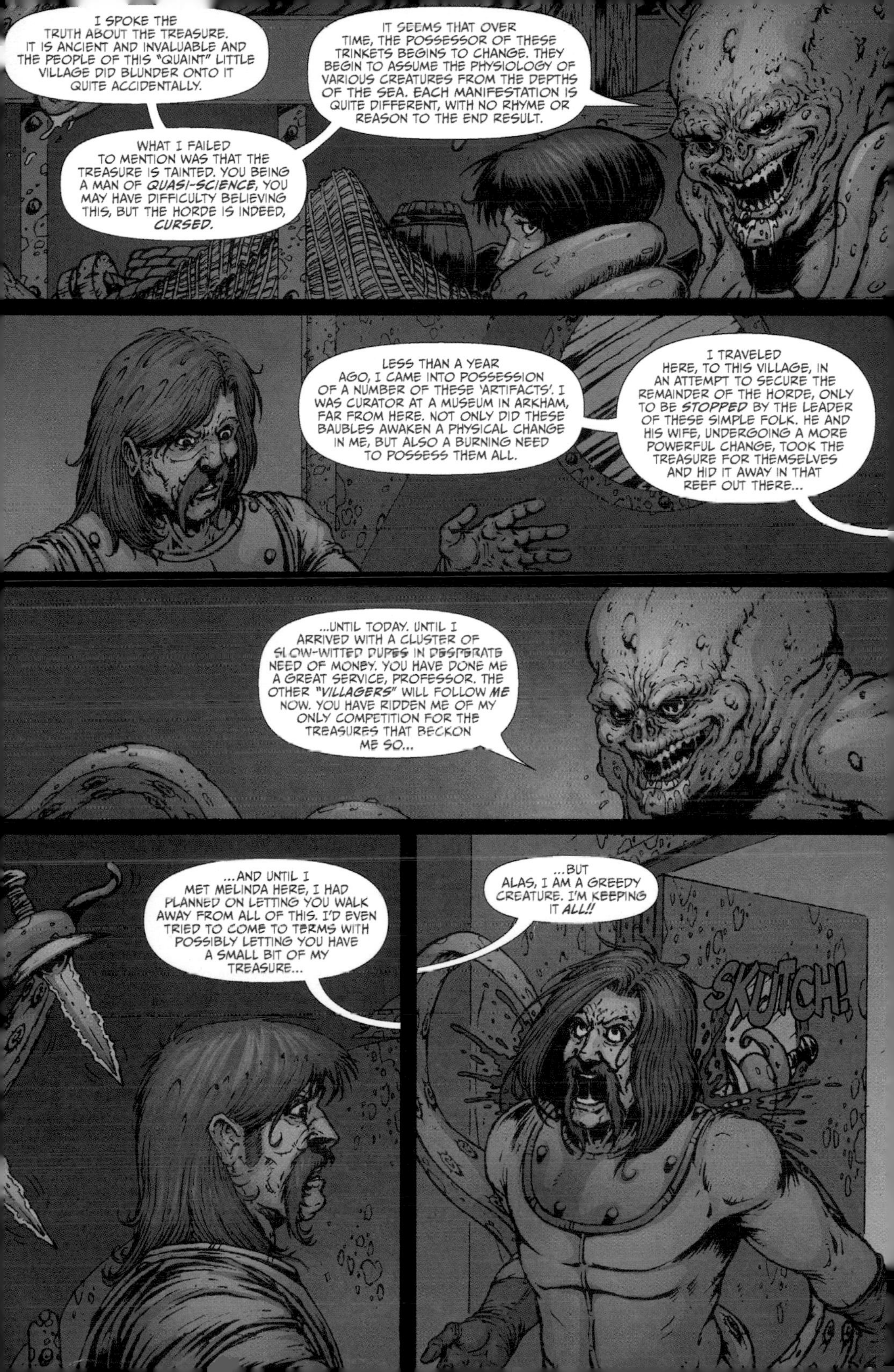
I SPOKE THE TRUTH ABOUT THE TREASURE. IT IS ANCIENT AND INVALUABLE AND THE PEOPLE OF THIS "QUAINT" LITTLE VILLAGE DID BLUNDER ONTO IT QUITE ACCIDENTALLY.
WHAT I FAILED TO MENTION WAS THAT THE TREASURE IS TAINTED. YOU BEING A MAN OF QUASI-SCIENCE, YOU MAY HAVE DIFFICULTY BELIEVING THIS, BUT THE HORDE IS INDEED, CURSED.
IT SEEMS THAT OVER TIME, THE POSSESSOR OF THESE TRINKETS BEGINS TO CHANGE. THEY BEGIN TO ASSUME THE PHYSIOLOGY OF VARIOUS CREATURES FROM THE DEPTHS OF THE SEA. EACH MANIFESTATION IS QUITE DIFFERENT, WITH NO RHYME OR REASON TO THE END RESULT.
LESS THAN A YEAR AGO, I CAME INTO POSSESSION OF A NUMBER OF THESE 'ARTIFACTS'. I WAS CURATOR AT A MUSEUM IN ARKHAM, FAR FROM HERE. NOT ONLY DID THESE BAUBLES AWAKEN A PHYSICAL CHANGE IN ME, BUT ALSO A BURNING NEED TO POSSESS THEM ALL.
I TRAVELED HERE, TO THIS VILLAGE, IN AN ATTEMPT TO SECURE THE REMAINDER OF THE HORDE, ONLY TO BE STOPPED BY THE LEADER OF THESE SIMPLE FOLK. HE AND HIS WIFE, UNDERGOING A MORE POWERFUL CHANGE, TOOK THE TREASURE FOR THEMSELVES AND HID IT AWAY IN THAT REEF OUT THERE...
...UNTIL TODAY. UNTIL I ARRIVED WITH A CLUSTER OF SLOW-WITTED DUPES IN DESPERATE NEED OF MONEY. YOU HAVE DONE ME A GREAT SERVICE, PROFESSOR. THE OTHER "VILLAGERS" WILL FOLLOW ME NOW. YOU HAVE RIDDEN ME OF MY ONLY COMPETITION FOR THE TREASURES THAT BECKON ME SO...
...AND UNTIL I MET MELINDA HERE, I HAD PLANNED ON LETTING YOU WALK AWAY FROM ALL OF THIS. I'D EVEN TRIED TO COME TO TERMS WITH POSSIBLY LETTING YOU HAVE A SMALL BIT OF MY TREASURE...
...BUT ALAS, I AM A GREEDY CREATURE. I'M KEEPING IT ALL!!
SKUTCH!

MIDNIGHT...

CHUG-CHUG-CHUG-CHUG

CHUG
CHUG
CHUG
CHUG

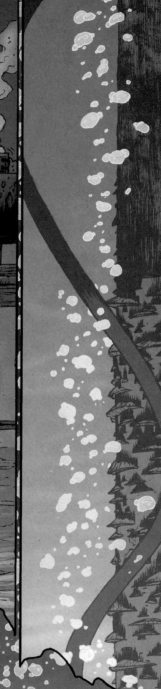

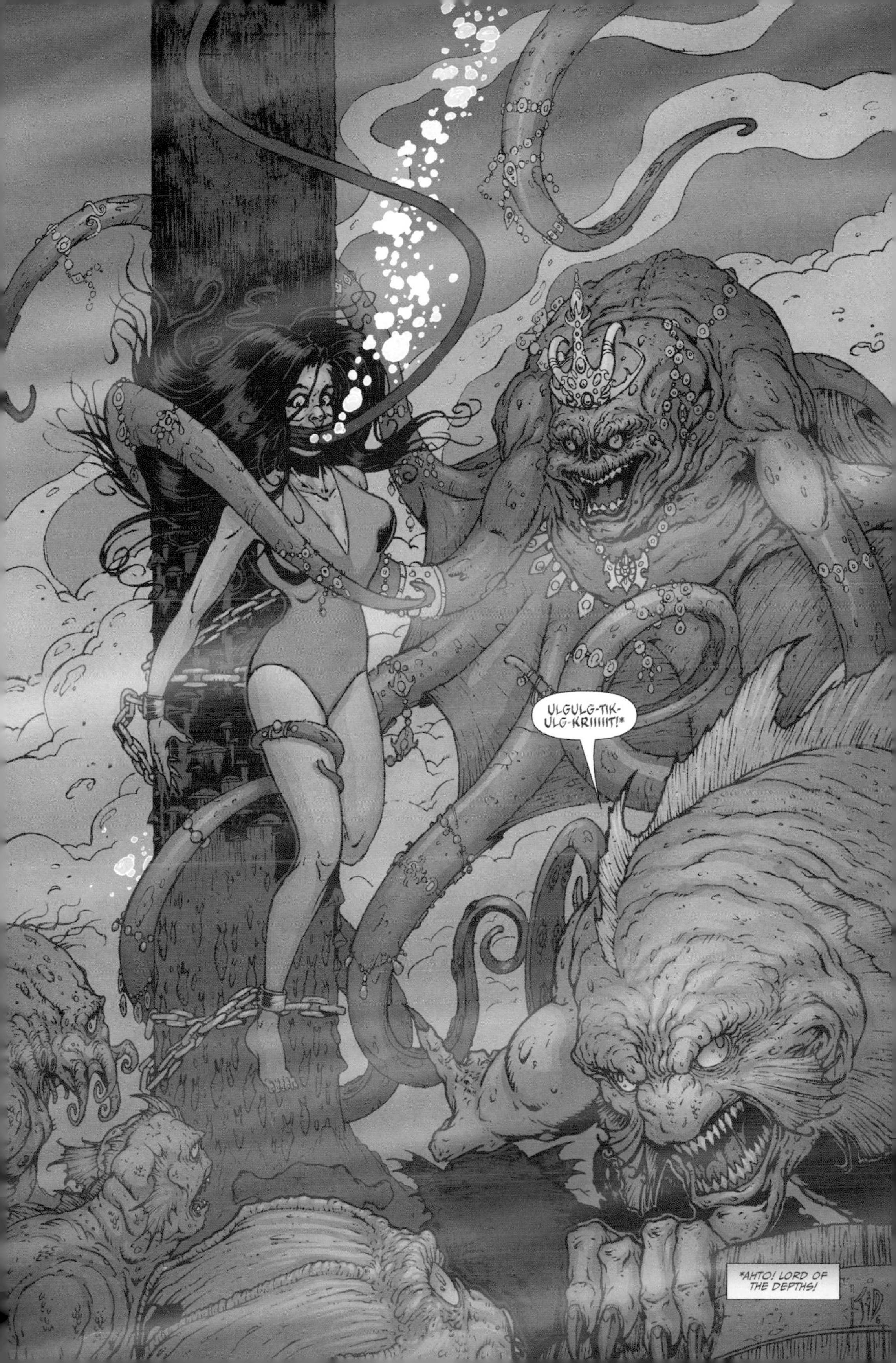
ULGULG-TIK-ULG-KRIIIIIT!*
*AHTO! LORD OF THE DEPTHS!

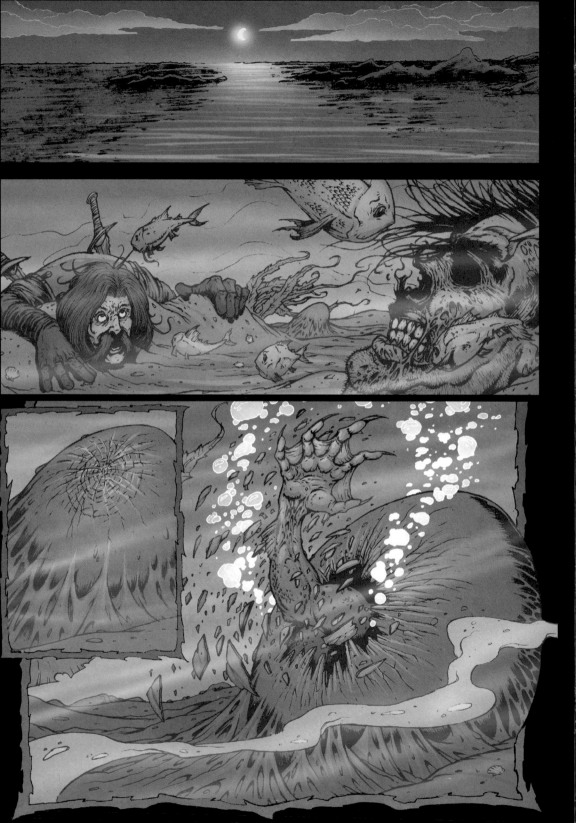

Howard Phillips Lovecraft

Howard Phillips Lovecraft was born on August 20, 1890, in Providence, Rhode Island. His father was Winfield Scott Lovecraft, a traveling salesman. His mother was Sarah Susan Phillips Lovecraft.

Lovecraft was a bright child. He could recite poetry at age two and read at age three. As a boy Lovecraft was often ill. When he was able to, he attended the Slater Avenue School. He later attended Hope Street High School but did not graduate.

Lovecraft learned mostly through reading on his own. His first printed work appeared in 1906. It was a letter to *The Providence Sunday Journal*. From 1906 to 1918, he wrote monthly astronomy columns for several other papers.

Lovecraft also composed poetry and fiction. His writing became popular when several short stories were accepted by *Weird Tales*, the pulp magazine. He soon was known as a writer of weird fiction.

On March 15, 1937, H.P. Lovecraft died after battling intestinal cancer. Today, he is often acknowledged as the inventor of modern horror. His works have inspired Wes Craven, Stephen King, and many other authors.

Lovecraft Has Many Additional Works Including

The Mysterious Ship (1902)

The Beast in the Cave (1905)

The Alchemist (1908)

Dagon (1917)

The Tomb (1917)

The Cats of Ulthar (1920)

The Dream-Quest of Unknown Kadath (1927)

The Case of Charles Dexter Ward (1927)

At the Mountains of Madness (1931)

The Dreams in the Witch House (1932)

Glossary

affliction - illness that causes continuous pain or anguish.

antiquity - early historical times, especially before the AD 500s. Antiquities are the objects, such as art and architecture, from those times.

curator - a person in charge of a place that has exhibits, such as a museum or zoo.

hamlet - a small village.

Piscean - fishy. Pisces is the Latin word for fishes.

proposition - something offered for consideration or acceptance.

quaint - something that is old-fashioned in a pleasing way.

Web Sites

To learn more about H.P. Lovecraft, visit ABDO Publishing Company on the World Wide Web at **www.abdopublishing.com**. Web sites about Lovecraft are featured on our Book Links page. These links are routinely monitored and updated to provide the most current information available.

3 1125 00731 5714